TALES TOLD AT MIDNIGHT

Liam A. Spinage

TALES TOLD AT MIDNIGHT

GRAVESTONE PRESS

Contents

Contents

In The Detail

Letitia stood alone on the balcony, glass in hand, looking out over the night sky. Far below her was the swirling fog of city lights: neon signs, headlamps, streetlights. Mere pinpricks at this distance but they melded together in a medley of memories. There had been times when she had been behind one of those lights, like so many other people in the city and not detached from it here in the penthouse. She swirled the champagne in the flute, sending bubbles scattering like flies. The sweet glass of victory twinkled in the suffused glow of the apartment lighting and the candle she had precariously balanced on the balcony table next to her, sputtering in the breeze but remaining defiant. She felt a lot of empathy for that candle. A tiny, exhaustible flicker of passion against a sky of brooding, monotonous darkness.

Still lost in thought, she took a tentative sip, relishing the cool feeling as it trickled down her throat. The rest of the bottle sat on the table next to the candle, still chilling in the ice bucket. She would save that for later. There were reasons to celebrate tonight, but the past five years had installed within her a certain degree of caution. Not for the first time but maybe - just maybe - for the last, she reflected on that momentous decision five years ago which had fundamentally changed her life.

The door buzzer sounded from deep within the apartment. She paused for a moment, but the buzzer did not. She usually had someone to deal with these interruptions, but she had dismissed her staff for the evening so that she would not be disturbed - except by him, obviously - though she hadn't thought he would approach in such a mundane way. A puff of smoke, maybe, a whiff of sulfur, a flash of bright flame, but no, he was about to enter in the same way that everyone else did.

She reached towards the white marble table and delicately deposited her glass there. Then she began to make her way back through her spacious lodgings. A four-poster bed with white satin drapes and twinkling dimmed fairy lights for that otherworldly feel. A spotless lounge, floored in white polished marble and a single small but perfectly placed rug. Busts of Medea, Circe and Ariadne sourced from the finest auction houses in the city and the world beyond, an entry room with a spacious cloakroom to one side, hidden behind black velvet curtains. Effortlessly, she raised a manicured finger and released the latch. As the handle turned, she paced back into the lounge and struck a pose on the scarlet chaise longue opposite the overstuffed armchair. That was the single item of furniture which stuck out in her otherwise immaculately appointed paradise, and it was here for a reason. It was the only memory she allowed herself from her former life. Until now.

She could hear his footsteps and the click of his cane approaching. *Something wicked this way comes.* A moment of rustling where he had clearly divested himself of an outer garment in the allotted place, A rushing intake of breath as he surveyed the sheer majesty of what he had helped her to afford. As he approached, Letitia faltered for a moment. His very presence drew her back to that time when they had first met, when the power difference between them had been so very different. The sheer malignancy of that shadow, even when dressed in human form, drew her in like a moth to a flame. For the first time, she began to wonder whether the strategy she had devised would work. She shivered, trembled even at every footstep until she glimpsed herself momentarily in the mirror and saw her younger self, high on life, drunk on her own confidence, about to make what could easily be the biggest and most dangerous mistake of her life. She barely recognized that young girl in herself after all this time. She was different now. Not just richer, but more mature, more experienced. Her inner confidence grew, and she regained her composure just as he spoke to her.

"Good evening. I see you were expecting me." His voice, low but sonorous, more than a hint of mischief, the same as it had been five years ago.

Finally, she turned to meet his face. Though she was sure it was just the same after all this time, the balance between them had shifted slightly. That face had haunted and taunted her over the years, reflected in dozens of shop windows, revolving doors, cocktail glasses, champagne flutes. Was it just her imagination or had he been with her every step of the way, looking, laughing, crowing, waiting... Just how much of her life did he know?

The face was still long and lean. In the light of the bar where they had first met, it had been sweaty,

9

sallow even, yet still handsome. That's what had first attracted her to him. His lashes, his moustaches. There were few well-groomed and well-dressed individuals in that dive. She had instantly wanted to know his story. He, in turn, had instantly wanted to know hers. The night had passed slowly, exchanges between them became more friendly, more fervent. Then, as she gazed into his hypnotizing grey eyes, he had made her an offer she couldn't refuse.

"Hello, you old devil. Has it really been five years?"

His face was different now, she realized. The line of his lips which had once been so willing to laugh now formed a sneer, giving way as he spoke to betray the immense hunger behind those perfect white teeth. She instinctively gulped, trying not to show it. If she showed fear now, all would be lost.

"It has. As you well know. And now I arrive at the appointed hour to collect what is due. I see that you have been enjoying your gift." He extended an arm sleeved in a dark suit - charcoal grey, she thought in the dim light, with a flash of bright red lining - as a sweep around the penthouse.

"I have not forgotten. Please, sit." She gestured at the cracked leather of the armchair. He bowed slightly, mockingly, and did so.

"I'm here to collect, waitress."

She laughed, deep and rich and long. He joined in.

"It's been a long time since I've been that, but still, I have a memory of that night when we first met, see? You're sitting on it. That's the armchair

10

from the staff break room where you sat as I poured out my hopes and fears and you offered me the world on a plate. A simple transaction, really." Was it her imagination or did he actually begin to look uncomfortable? Had he perhaps an inkling of what was about to happen?

"I recall it well, waitress."

Well. To be addressed in that manner a second time was simply rude. Not that she considered the devil above petty manipulation, far from it. He was trying to put her off-kilter. Playing with his food before he devoured her utterly.

"Do you also recall…" she tailed off, lost for a moment in the handsomeness of his lean face, those hungry eyes, that perfect chin. "Do you recall what it was I asked of you?"

"I do, but I don't need to. It's all here." From the interior of his suit jacket, he withdrew a single piece of paper and let it unfurl, first from his wrist to the arm of the chair and then across the floor, stopping finally at the outline of the rug. "Second thoughts, waitress? It's a little too late for that. Five years too late, I should say. Don't be coy. You accepted the gift, now accept the consequences." He leaned forward in a gesture of quiet menace clearly honed by what she imagined was millennia of practice. Behind him on the wall, his shadow loomed large even while he remained seated. Though her rooms were lit with the brightest lamps, the shadow he cast now - and the shadow he had cast over her life for the last five years - threatened to drown her in darkness.

"Yes. Success. That's what I traded my soul for. Success in my chosen occupation. And that has worked out very well for me, very well indeed, I must agree. I have the world at my feet." She stood quietly, in one lithe movement, her pearls swaying slowly at her alabaster throat.

"There must be a particular thirst for cocktails that I was unaware of at the time. Who would have thought!"

She moved in stockinged feet to the scroll now fully unfurled across the room and removed an elegant pair of glasses from a case in her purse. He seemed to anticipate this move.

"They always think there's something in the contract that can get them out." This was barely perceptible to Letitia, almost a mutter, but it echoed nevertheless around the empty space between them and hung, lingering in the air with a faint whiff of threat and sulfur. He spoke it as if an aside to a hidden third party. Or perhaps to himself, a mote of contempt for his victims which he had only vocalized so that she could feel the cruel, casual mockery in his voice.

"Oh, I'm sure many have tried!" She attempted a laugh, but it came out a little hoarse, a little stilted. He was beginning to sense her fear. "It's quite clear though, you're right." She knelt down before the lengthy contract and squinted briefly at the small print before beginning to read the first line. "I, Letitia Maria de Santis do, on this day of November 27th 1981, at the hour of 3 AM, enter into this agreement whereby I will be granted unparalleled success in my chosen profession for five years in

12

return for which at the appointed hour five years from now I will relinquish my soul to the devil in payment," She shot a glance across at him over the rim of her glasses delicately balanced on the bridge of her nose. On the mantle, perched between two alabaster busts, a golden clock ticked slowly, irrevocably, towards that very hour.

"So?" He rubbed his hands together in glee. "What are we waiting for?"

"It's the small print that interests me."

"Oh?" He appeared unperturbed. "Most people don't even give that a second glance. I mean, what's a few extra words in comparison to five years of fame and riches?"

"Is it always five years?" The question seemed to shock him a little and he tilted his head a little, his brows raised quizzically.

"It is traditional, yes. Just enough rope for people to hang themselves with, you see. Oh, I know..." here he brushed off a little yellow dust from his shoulder as easily as he brushed off her question, "I know that fifteen minutes of fame was all the rage some while back, but what we savor is the anticipation of doom that a contract end represents. Why, you wouldn't believe the lengths some people go to trying to get out of the deal. Or maybe you would?" At that last line, the inflection in his voice changed slightly, becoming more contemplative. Then he laughed again, and the moment was lost. "You're not trying to negotiate an extension, are you? Oh, how simply delightful It won't work I'm afraid."

"And yet there is nothing here in any of the subclauses which necessarily precludes such an arrangement, I thought it at least worth a try."

"Sorry." He was not sorry. He was not an entity for which remorse, repentance or forgiveness could even exist. The word was a mere formality, an amuse-bouche to whet his appetite before his lean form sprang forward, pouncing voraciously on his trapped prey. "But when your number's up…"

"Yes, I understand". She got back to her feet and walked over to a cabinet on the far side of the room, flinging open the doors. "Still, it seems that at least I can offer you a drink while you're here?" The chair creaked as he turned it around slightly, arching his back to take in the full display of bottles available. There must have been over a hundred there, all manner of shapes and sizes, antique bottles covered in dust, cut glass carafes full of unknown concoctions, shiny new bottles of the most expensive spirits affordable on earth.

"I will take one cocktail of your choosing, to humor you. After all, when you've been instrumental in making the career of the finest cocktail waitress in the world, it's a bonus to see what you have helped achieve."

"Very well. Allow me." Letitia busied herself for some moments, unstopping some bottles and inspecting the contents. Finally, she began pouring small measures into a cocktail shaker and then reached into the cabinet and extracted two highball glasses. He seemed content to watch her in those silent moments, savoring the last hours of her life before he claimed it for eternity.

Turning her back on him - especially at such a critical juncture - might have been perceived as a power move. Certainly, Letitia could feel her power growing, though her hands still shook slightly as she uncorked a large bottle of fortified wine. Perhaps, just perhaps, this might actually work. Hiding her fear, she nevertheless wanted to know how he saw her at that moment. Was she still prey? Or, just maybe, boon companion? Dare she even imagine…adversary?

She could see him out of the corner of her eye, just about, but more keenly in the many reflective surfaces of the bottles arrayed before her. His lean figure, at ease in the armchair, his eager face watching her back, reflected and distorted by the different folds and twists in the antique bottles which lined the cabinet. His visage tinted blue here, green there from the contents of those bottles, elongated almost beyond recognition by the cut of the crystal decanters, fractured into multiple facades by the refraction of the light through the water, each proffering a different promise. But in each of them, clear as anything, were the glint of those grey, uncompromising, all-seeing eyes.

Finally, her task complete, she added an olive and a twist to each then made her way back to the chaise longue. Leaning over, she proffered him one of the glasses with a final flourishing swirl. The clear liquid sprang into life as hues of red and yellow began swirling around each other as if in mutual pursuit.

15

"Very clever!" He raised the glass to his ruby lips, taking in the heady aroma. Letitia mirrored the procedure.

"To us! Success at a price."

"To us!"

He took his first swallow of whatever deliciousness she had prepared, Letitia herself hesitated for a moment before she swallowed, waiting to see his reaction,

He began spluttering almost immediately, the liquid spraying from his mouth as he started to cough, Letitia looked over, knowingly.

"What have you done? That was awful! Probably the worst thing I've ever tasted!" When he had recovered a little of his form, he reached into his jacket for a slate-grey silk handkerchief which, she noted, was even monogrammed with a little red 'L' in the corner. He held it to his lips, still occasionally retching, and wiped the spittle from his chin,

"I never was any good at making cocktails."

"What? I made you the best in the world! What have you done with that? How have you got all this wealth from so little talent?"

"I direct you again to the terms of our contract."

"I... What? You wanted to be the best at your chosen profession. What happened?"

"Correct. But that chosen profession wasn't making cocktails. I was only doing that to make ends meet during my studies. My chosen profession was contract law." She sipped at her own cocktail, unstirred, and looked back at him with an expression that was half-grimace, half-grin. "I do apologize if that happens to be a matter of confusion

16

for you. The way the contract is worded wasn't specific about that, you see." She leaned forward conspiratorially, confident in her approach now. "But we can change that, you and I."

He could feel the power between them shifting slightly. He didn't like it.

"I'm quite sure I don't know what you mean."

"I mean that it's still possible for me to negotiate an extension. Now, you, as the party of the first part…"

"Wait, wait." He seemed to need time to think. Letitia thought this was amusing and her mouth betrayed the tiniest of smirks. But it wasn't over yet. Even as the balance between them began to tip in her favor, she couldn't afford to let it show fully. Still, she enjoyed watching him squirm as she swilled the contents of her glass. When she saw her own reflection in that glass, and his too, hovering on the edge, she was struck at the similarity between them. She looked up.

"Why wait? By accident, it seems that you have created the finest contract lawyer on earth. That's what has brought me all this fame, all these lovely curios, this wonderful penthouse apartment. You thought I got all this from inventing some new drink? Please. If I understand correctly - and here the print is quite clear - when I go with you then all this is over. All the gifts offered, this keen mind, this knowledge, are lost to me and you both. It's also clear that despite all rumor to the contrary, hell really does not have all the best lawyers. There are clauses here that are so ridiculously archaic as to be meaningless. Surely you would appreciate my insights into it before you take your prize back with you for an infinity of torture?"

As pitches go, she thought she'd nailed it. He seemed to agree, but then a wry smile took over his face again. "What you suggest should take no more than five hours, let alone five more years. Nevertheless, I concur. Fix me something that's actually palatable and let us both take a look at the fine print together. Maybe you really can teach this old dog some new tricks."

Three hours later, they looked up from a second contract, with even more confounding legalese and clauses than the devil could hope for. Vials of red and black ink lie strewn across the cold marble of the floor and the teak writing desk; a feather had escaped from a quill and was slowly meandering across the floor toward the balcony in a breeze-borne bid for freedom.

"Well." He stood straight and tall. "That is certainly an improvement. I cannot thank you enough."

Letitia raised a single perfectly plucked eyebrow. He laughed, "A mere figure of speech, something I am certain never to write down." He sobered again and extended a long bony hand toward her. "Now, come. You are done with this world."

"Oh, I don't think so." Letitia drained a tiny cup heavy with caffeine stains. She also stood, stretching as she did so. For the first time, she looked him in the eye and did not blink. Then she picked up her contract again and slowly crossed the space between them, her stockinged feet silent on the marble floor. The devil may be in the detail, but this line of the contract is just heavenly." She pursed her lips to proffer a kiss into the air. "*In return for which, at the appointed hour*. I'm afraid to break it to you, but that appointed hour has come and gone." Her eyes flicked briefly back to the clock on the mantle.

Letitia handed him the contract which he started at, dumbfounded, as she moved lithely across the room, stopping in front of her bedroom door. "It is now eight in the morning." With that, she threw open the door with a flourish, flooding the room with light from the balcony beyond. "The sun has risen while you made work for my idle hands. All those extra clauses. Dear me. I'll have to leave you now." She squinted through the door to her bedroom and the balcony where the sun had risen magnificently. "I have an appointment with another morning star. I'm sure you can find your own way out."

Leaving the devil howling in frustrated rage, Letitia walked out into the light and poured herself another glass of champagne. She never had liked cocktails.

These Poor Compounds

"Exhibit A, an empty glass vial with a torn plain label." The podestà nods to the clerk, who, having placed the exhibit carefully before them, takes a seat in the corner of the wood-paneled room next to the door. The podestà turns his overly large, lop-sided head to the wretch standing at the lectern before him.

"Please, do tell me what this substance is."

The apothecary, rag-clad and bushy-browed, squints in the half-light of the candlelit courtroom.

"It is a substance I hath sold only once, for the price of forty ducats, to one noble youth these three days past."

The podestà nods even as the crowd gasps. With a withering glance, he quiets the room. This is his space: he will brook no interruption from the throng there assembled.

"And pray, good sir, what is the nature of this substance?" He knows the answer. The horrific scenes at the tomb made it perfectly obvious what the compound was designed to do.

The apothecary shifts slightly on his feet and swallows deeply. He knows his time is short now, as it always is for those unfortunate common souls who are caught up in the affairs of nobles. If only that deluded youth had not sought him out and pressured him into a sale. With eyes closed and head bowed in shame, he speaks the words he knows will condemn him to a death without mercy and an eternity of damnation.

"It is pure poison, my lord. A poison so puissant that one dose would fell twenty men."

There is another round of gasps from the gallery, surprised at the affrontery of this squalid, common merchant to be involved in the trade of such things. The podestà contemplates ordering it cleared, but those who pay his keep are contained there and it would not do to deny them their pound of flesh. Besides, he has another, more important, concern. Namely, that this was not the answer he had anticipated. Desperately trying to contain his surprise while also silencing the room, he turns back to the wretched vendor wringing his wizened, liver-spotted hands in the dock.

"It is not, then, a compound traditionally associated with the dark art of necromancy?"

Now it is the apothecary's turn to look surprised. He makes the sign of the cross and visibly shrinks in fear, backing off as if the substance were laid directly under his nose. Meanwhile, the good Friar Laurence, leaning over the railing from the public gallery, clenches it so tightly he fears it would collapse and send him plummeting to the ground. He fervently hopes the podestà doesn't need to interrogate him: he knows he won't be able to lie under oath.

"Dear me! Nay, my lord, it is not such a hideous concoction. Merely a compound of poisons." The apothecary shuffles on his aching feet, favoring now the right leg which pains him considerably less. Internally, he is relieved. They have made a mistake, one that seems to vindicate him. Might they overlook his testimony and grant him release? He offers a further prayer, muttered in the silence of the courtroom.

Friar Laurence feels sorry for the apothecary, begins to fret, and tugs at his rosary. If only there was a way to free this poor soul without incriminating himself.

The podestà nods but narrows his eyes accusingly. He's not done yet. "Call the first witness."

A young sergeant stands and shuffles slowly forward, holding before him a large package wrapped in stained silk. His bearing is stiff and formal, though his head droops a little and his eyes, accustomed to being alert, are bloodshot and bleary. He is sworn in with a flurry of hurried Latin. The podestà knows him, he's been serving in the birri for three long years, but all the fear and hopelessness in his face speaks only to the incident that occurred just three nights ago.

"He is lost to us. Maybe the priesthood will take him in. I shall make enquiries. Such a loss to the profession." This is what the podestà is thinking, but what he says is: "Please explain to the court, in your own words, the sequence of events for the night in question."

The sergeant stands bold upright, leaves the parcel on the requisite evidence table, and begins to relate the terrible tale from memory, interspersed intermittently to take slow, deliberate draughts of the watered wine, lifted to his haggard face with trembling arms.

"We were on routine patrol when we heard a disturbance near the Capulet tomb." He delivers his first line without hesitation but begins to stammer as he continues.

***

"Sergeant!"

The young man turns on his heels, delivering a swift quick to the nearest creature in the process. In all his active life policing, he has never seen a scene like this. He prays he never will again.

"Sergeant, there are five more approaching from the tomb!"

He utters an oath under his breath, swearing that he will repent all his sins and take up holy orders if only he survives this night.

"The captain has set a fire at the north end of the valley. Lead them there!"

"Burn the corpses?" It is a moment of incredulity, a command which goes against everything he has been taught. The sergeant too.

"Do it!" The sergeant responds more urgently now, deftly parrying a rapier blow which comes lightning fast from the ... thing he now faces. In life, judging by the fashionable apparel, this might easily have been a noble youth, desperate to prove himself. As what remains of him shuffles, salivates, and swipes its way around his defensive posture, the sergeant wonders what unholy powers have been at work here to deliver this half-alive, half-dead monstrosity. The expression on its pale face is snarling hatred, though its eyes are soulless and vacant. What remains of the fine doublet have been cut by a dozen ineffective thrusts of his own rapier,

23

exposing long claw marks on its taut, tanned flesh that must have been made by another of its kind - and recently, because there were no disturbances at the tomb on the previous evening when the lady Juliet had been laid to rest. He'd been there himself to supervise and offered condolences to the doomed girl's good mother. He'd assured her that the tomb would be guarded. He hoped he would never have to look into that tear-stained, grief-stricken face again and tell her just how badly he had failed.

Yet there she was, he realized, shuffling towards him on wounded knees, her dress ripped and covered in mud but unmistakably her fashion. Whilst his troops rallied to their captain and his blasphemous pyre, he now had two walking corpses to contend with. Lady Capulet and what was presumably one of her family.

***

"We…we had to burn many of them." A slight pause in his testimony while he looked up at the good friar on the balcony. "We also had to burn those of ours that fell to their onslaught, because as they did, they rose again. So help me God, they rose again." The sergeant empties the glass beside him in a single gulp; its contents are instantly replaced by the invisible hands of the courtroom staff.

"Continue, sergeant. You have conducted yourself admirably in your retelling thus far."

A rattling cough. A shaking hand. A deadness to the eyes. For a brief second, the sergeant is indistinguishable from the walking dead in his own waking nightmare. Then, the comparison ends, and he takes up the tale further.

24

"I had evaded the two which assailed me and took up a defensive position in the Capulet tomb itself. Here were buried the noble dead of many centuries…"

***

The sergeant kneels on the dank stone floor of the tomb next to another body. He doesn't think this one shows any signs of moving, and he is watching very, very closely for any sign of life as he investigates the wounds on the youth's torso and arms. A detailed inspection reveals they have all been caused by swordplay. Particularly, they all seem to have been caused by the same sword, in the same fight. He makes a mental note of this, somehow what happened here must be important to the disastrous situation which the captain and the other birri are facing outside. It must be, otherwise he has come into the eye of the storm for no reason other than to die and he could have achieved that by fighting back-to-back with his comrades in the commotion further down the valley, or any other night on the dangerous streets of Verona.

He shoots a second glance at this particular body - Paris by name according to the locket around his neck - still unconvinced that it has no intentions of struggling to its feet and lurch forward with a blood-chilling moan, eager to sink its teeth and hands into his flesh. He has already been unfooted and unhinged by that twice on this foulest of nights and has thus vowed never to be fooled again. Flaming torch in hand and rapier held before him in the other, he descends the steps into the family tomb of the Capulets where he hopes to discover just how the tragedies and horrors of this night might have unfolded.

***

"I discovered two bodies in an alcove there, entwined in death as in life." The first, a youth known to us now as one Romeo Montague."

"Silence, I say again!" The sergeant looks up, startled, as the podestà makes a further attempt at shushing the crowd on the balcony. "Once more and I shall have you dismissed! I will brook no interruption in this courtroom. Am I clear?" The ensuing silence appears to indicate the positive.

"Sergeant, please continue."

"There are no tooth or claw wounds on this body, only sword-wounds, similar to the body I found outside. It is my deduction that this youth, for reasons unknown, dueled with that second and won, then entered the tomb."

The podestà nods, though inside his head is shaking with sorrow. He knows the course of events which has been playing out across the plazas and streets of Verona only too well. These youths spent in futile warfare; their days and nights fueled by an ancient grudge; their brightly burning lives now extinguished by a compound of errors. Capulet and Montague, two households, both alike in death. With a wave of his hand, he permits the sergeant to speak again.

"It is from the hand of this youth, Romeo, that I retrieved Exhibit A, which has already been discussed." Friar Lawrence, still clinging to the balcony for dear life with white-knuckled hands, near faints at the news. "The second body within the

26

tomb is that of the young lady, Juliet, identifiable both from the locket in Paris' possession and from the simple fact that it is her tomb which we were sent to guard, since she had died and been placed there a day hence. Her lips, like those of Romeo, bear a slight blue tinge, from which I deduce that she has also supped from the contents of Exhibit A. Her teeth are also stained with blood and inside her mouth I discovered fragments of human flesh. The overall pattern of her teeth matches the bite marks on the upper arm of the body of the deceased Lady Capulet, which is presented in evidence to the court as Exhibit B."

If the tumult from the public balcony had risen to an ungodly level before, the clamor from that place now carried sounds straight from the depths of Hell itself. There were several ear-piercing screams as the cloth was removed from Exhibit B next to the sergeant. Two onlookers, possessing a more fragile constitution than their counterparts, fainted dead away. Three more tried to violently exit the door all at the same time and fell about each other in a rush to reach the fresher air of the street. While this continued, the podestà realized, the investigation itself could not go on. The presentation of part of a dead body itself would not normally cause such consternation, even when victim and watcher alike were both of a sensitive noble stock unaccustomed to the rambunctiousness of a courtroom. It is at that moment that he realizes something else is going very wrong.

The arm writhes as it is uncovered. Slowly at first, as if stretching after an afternoon nap in the warm sun, flexing its blood-crusted fingers and mud-caked nails. Of its own hellish volition, it twitches violently, knocking over the evidence stand on which it sits, then spasms several times on the hard wooden floor before lurching itself with vigor at the sergeant's neck. The three who tried to leave are still blocking the exit with their irrelevant argument, but not for long. They are soon swept under the feet of a deluge of desertion, a rout of reason, as in desperation all those who had come to see the outcome of the trial of a simple apothecary run from the place, crushing the three obstreperous men before and beneath them.

Of that apothecary, one thing must now be said. Of all the people that remain in the court - and he could hardly leave, being clapped in irons - he displays in that moment the bravest heart and the quickest mind. Using his own hand irons as a trap, he confronts the cadaverous limb as it strangles the young sergeant and yanks it firmly away, only to be confronted with it himself. He manages to keep it at arm's length only with a fortitude drawn from a place deep within he knew not he possessed.

"The other compound!" His screech becomes a battle-cry. The sergeant rallies once he has recovered from the undead chokehold and uncorks a vial from the third stand beside him, which is labelled Exhibit C. "Pour it on the arm!" The apothecary's speech reaches fever-pitch as he tussles with the rancid clutches of the noble's blemished forearm. The sergeant does so without thinking and the corpse-arm shudders and then drops to the floor, finally dead.

"Your problem, podestà, is this second compound." The apothecary is half-gasping and half-ranting, all composure and servility now lost. "Whither it was gotten, I know not, though I know its desired effect. It should lay one peacefully to rest, which is to say to place one into a deep sleep, the brother of death. A simple fool such as I could make such a potion, were it permitted, and pass it onto another for a princely sum. That price would be more evil than the thing itself. For in compound with the first exhibit, it will bring first sleep, then a poisonous death and then a hungry death such as that described by the good sergeant. The action of giving this to, say, some young woman in pain, may be a civil act but it makes the civil hands unclean in retrospect."

Friar Lawrence places his head in his hands and sobs uncontrollably. He is escorted from the premises, but not before his picture is captured to be displayed and shamed upon the walls of the Bargello, to dwell in ignominious company among the pitturi infamiti whose portraits form a gallery of unlikely rogues.

The podestà sighs and the clerk steps forward with a third bottle. The label on this one is distinctive only to indicate the vintage. Three glasses are poured; the irons on the apothecary are removed.

Some, then, would be pardoned and some punished. A toast is raised and to a glooming peace the three survivors drink in turn.

"Here's to your love! Much good hath it wrought."

"Go hence, to have more talk of these sad things."

"Never was a story of more woe."

Hunger Stone

There are a number of black plastic sacks in the trunk of his car, and each contains a carefully wrapped human limb. That's probably all the information you need to identify the chosen career of James Patrick Devereaux.

That is, until today.

He stands on the edge of a reservoir, gripping the handrail with a hand fully encased in a soft pigskin driving glove. The other hand is busy dialing a stored number on his cellphone. A pair of powerful binoculars hangs from a leather cord around his slim, tanned neck. They sway slightly against the crisp whiteness of his shirt. For someone who has made a living the way he does, he looks distinctly perturbed about something. That is, he looks perturbed for him: it manifests only momentarily as a raised eyebrow, a slight scowl and the call he is about to make. Whatever the problem is, James is about to make it someone else's problem as well as his. He's that kind of guy.

"We got a problem." We. A problem shared is a problem halved.

The voice at the other end of the line is muffled. There's some shouting in the background, then a door slams shut and the voice becomes clearer.

"Hey, Paulie here. What's up?"

He briefly allows himself another scowl since nobody is watching. When this is over, he'll need to have words - again - about giving names over the phone. You'd think the mob would know better, but Paulie's old school.

"I need you to meet me immediately at Kensico Dam Plaza. I've sent the coordinates to your cell." No point in having a protracted conversation at this point. The problem will be obvious when Paulie gets here. James goes back to his car, closes the trunk and leans patiently against the driver's door until his guest arrives, reading the Wall Street Journal in the blazing sunshine without even raising a bead of sweat despite the heat and the impeccable tailored suit he still wears almost in defiance of it.

The same can't be said of Paulie when he arrives. He's every inch an old-style capo, three-piece Italian suit and expensive leather shoes. The suit jacket, though, is hanging over the seat of the car. Paulie - this is 'Big' Paulie, so there's just over five feet two of him - steps out, getting mud on his shoe. He curses and immediately lights a cigarette.

James sighs inwardly and makes another note to explain patiently about forensic evidence - again - at an appropriate time when Paulie won't just shout and spit in his face for five whole minutes. They've actually got more important business right now.

Paulie is perspiring profusely. Huge sweat pools are clearly visible under his arms and across his chest. He takes a handkerchief from his waistcoat pocket and mops his brow, as if that will make a difference other than to stop the sweat dripping into his eyes. His thinning hair is already plastered to his head. He wanders over as if he had all the time in the world.

32

"It's hot, huh?" Paulie states the obvious because he isn't much of a conversation starter and besides, he only knows who this guy is through his reputation, he's never met the famous fixer in person. He does know that he's on books for all the families in New York, that he's a serious player and not to fuck with him. But that doesn't lead to a character introduction or chit chat. He's been called here, for fuck's sake, he's not the one who should be doing the talking right now.

"97 degrees. Hottest the city has ever been. It's a little cooler out here, but it's still not good news."

"So, what am I doing here instead of standing in front of the big chest freezer in the ice cream parlor?" Paulie was irritated, running hot. It wasn't that he had anything specific to do, just that he'd rather not be doing this. He struggles to maintain composure. He is only here because if James calls, it means urgency, immediacy. At least, that's the service that was advertised. James has never called Paulie before. He hasn't needed to.

James, who was standing in front of a big freezer only a few hours ago, but for entirely different reasons, remains cool as a cucumber.

"Remember Danny Figaro? Used to sing his way through a hatchet job like he was auditioning to be an opera singer?"

"Ha, ha, yeah. I remember Danny. But he ain't a problem no more."

"I beg to differ."

Now Paulie really concentrated. If Danny wasn't dead, that was bad news. Not just because he'd be out for revenge, but because it means people have lied to him and Paulie really, really doesn't like it when people lie to him.

"Danny's gone, capice? Sleeping with the fishes."

"And where is it you think that fishes sleep?" James' tone is polite but inquisitorial.

"Huh?"

James raises his arms and looks around.

"Oh."

"It's been so hot and dry that on the River Po in Italy, decades-old shipwrecks have been resurfacing. We have a similar problem here. Look."

Paulie looks around for the first time, past James, over the railing and down into the reservoir. The water level is low. Dangerously low. Then it dawns on him.

"How many bodies we talking about?"

"At least six according to my records. Four of yours, one of Carlucci's and one of Moreno's. Plus, whatever or whoever got dumped here without my knowledge. If they're not already exposed - dislodged and carried to the edge - then in another couple of days, they will be. See that tunnel?" James offers Paulie the binoculars and points at a concrete pipe just above the surface which juts out of brown, parched rock spattered with a few hardy green weeds. Paulie nods. "That's the secondary exit overflow from the reservoir. It's supposed to provide the city with water. Now, what's wrong with this picture?"

"It's supposed to be underwater. Shit. Wait, what's that?"

"It's supposed to be *twenty feet* underwater. As to your question, I reckon that's the top half of a black plastic sack not unlike the ones I have in the trunk of my car."

"Shit. Shit shit shit."

"Quite."

"Wonder who the fuck that is."

"That is what I called you here to find out."

"Shit."

* * *

"Here's what I don't get. This place is important, right? Supplies the city with water?" Paulie has been listening to James explain how New York's water system works for over half an hour as the two of them climb, clamber, and slide their way down the steep banks of the reservoir. On the way, they'd passed different marks on the rocks which James said indicated where the water levels usually were. You could tell from the rocks and plants whether they were usually underwater or not. These rocks are slick, smooth with the gentle lapping of water over a hundred years or more. It makes it trickier to climb down and Paulie hasn't been that fit for a number of years now. Even without this heat, he'd be aching all over and wheezing right now. Even in this suffocating heat, James - who wasn't much younger but was certainly fitter - is visibly struggling and grunting.

"That's correct."

"Then why isn't it crawling with police already? Or Feds?"

James actually pauses to consider this, annoyed that he hadn't noticed the absence of law

35

enforcement himself, that he'd developed a chink in his armor that had allowed Paulie a well-placed blow. It was true that the place usually had a police presence. All the reservoir networks did, even those initial lakes that were actually well beyond traditional NYPD jurisdiction. He knows this partially because three of them are technically on his payroll. They look the other way when he needs them to, but what they don't do, apparently, is tip him off when something like this happens, something which threatens his clients. He'd had to discover it himself when he arrived here. He hadn't even had the presence of mind to realize himself what the heatwave might mean to reservoir levels. He manages a scowl, mostly at his own lack of foresight rather than directed at Paulie, before rallying himself to a riposte.

"You're right. There's usually a patrol, plus manned observation points around the lake. Let's proceed while we're not being watched. We can figure out what happened to them later."

Paulie is happy enough just to have got one over on James. Now they've reached the pipe entrance, he leans against the cool concrete of the tunnel, just out of the line of direct sunlight, to catch his breath, which he does by the absurd confabulation of panting and having another cigarette. James looks cautiously around the opening and prods the muddy bank with the remains of a sapling he's hauled out of the ground on the way down. This way, he manages to fish out three plastic sacks before Paulie has recovered enough to help him.

"So, who we got?" Paulie isn't big on we, doesn't budge an inch. He is, however, merrily poking around in the mud which, despite the heat, still pools in the cool shadows just beyond the tunnel entrance. It looks a lot bigger now they're standing directly in front of it: a well-worn circular passageway of solid concrete which leads into the side of the reservoir and slightly down. It gets dark pretty quick, and Paulie is using some antique cigarette lighter to illuminate a miniature fraction of the darkness within. James tosses him a flashlight.

"This one's Joey Manzini."

"Huh. Didn't even know about him."

"You're not the only one paying for my services." Spoken out loud it sounded curt - rude, even - but Paulie supposedly already knew this. They'd all signed off on it in one of those rare moments when they had all been in the same room and nobody had immediately started shouting at each other. The good old days.

"It's definitely him. There's a serial number on the blue plastic handles of each bag, if you know where to look. Trust me, unless someone has been up here and switched body parts among different bags - after they've already been given concrete shoes and without me knowing, - it can't be anyone else."

"Hey, look at this." Paulie had been waving the flashlight around in the entrance, sending rays of light into the subterranean gloom like a kid playing with a new toy. The beam strikes a flagstone in the tunnel floor which isn't slick with slime like the others. It remains a soft, dull gray.

James, his identification work done for the time being, walks over. If nothing else, humor the guy. No point getting on his bad side.

"What is it?"

"Writing. In Latin. Si videries me lamentate. Huh?"

James fumbles with his phone. "Hold up a sec. I'll pop that through google translate."

"I know what it translates to. *If you see me, weep.* I just don't get it."

"It's a hunger stone. They've been spotted in the Elbe and other rivers in this year's drought." James doesn't dwell on the intensity of the Catholic upbringing necessary to translate Latin in the field. He doesn't need to because Paulie is busy tugging at the little silver crucifix around his scrawny, liver-spotted neck. "Supposedly, they were used to mark desperately low river levels that would forecast famines. Odd to see one in a reservoir that wasn't constructed until the late 1800s."

Paulie doesn't miss a beat to wonder how James knows this shit either. As far as he understands it, it's literally James' job to know weird shit like this.

What neither of them know, though, is what the sign underneath the message means. It's been etched hard into the stone with a more coarse instrument than the precision of the text and it looks exactly like a kid's crude crayon drawing of a branch, surrounded by smudged squiggles which look meaningless but kind of make your head hurt if you try and focus on them for too long, Paulie is finding this out the hard way while James takes photos on his phone camera.

Paulie stands, woozy, and staggers back into the sunlight where he retches a few times and then leans against the entrance again. James goes deeper, not by much, and Paulie sees a few flashes of light coming from the tunnel and a couple of scuffling noises. Then he comes out, dragging the flagstone in one hand and a small black plastic bag in the other.

"Give me a hand with this." James keeps the bag and Paulie takes the weight of the uprooted stone.

"And just what are we going to do with that?"

"Get it to an expert. Something weird is going on here and I've got a hunch that crop failure wasn't the thing the hunger stone was meant to warn people about."

"And what makes you think that?" Paulie's expression shows a modicum of curiosity, no fear, and a little annoyance at having to do some heavy lifting, presumably all the way to the lip of the reservoir back to their cars.

"Call me cynical," James quips as he holds open the bin bag so Paulie can get a look, "but at a guess I'd say it's the desiccated remains of at least two NYPD officers." Paulie recoils, retches again and then gathers himself. He's glad the only thing he's carrying back to the car is a heavy stone inscribed with arcane gobbledygook.

***

They decide to take Paulie's car, on account of James' car already having most of a dead body in it. Paulie drives, naturally. James broods silently in the passenger seat. Neither of them wants to talk about what might be going on, but it's clear after a few minutes of silence that there's nothing else for them to talk about.

"So, any idea what those symbols are?" Paulie fires the opening shot.

James shakes his head. In comparison to his usual stoic-slash-pensive, this makes him positively fidgety. "Not a clue. Not my wheelhouse. I have to admit being stumped on that matter. I'm going through all the ramifications, though. Potential action plans and ways we could proceed. The original problem hasn't gone away, but we need to get this angle sorted before we can reduce ourselves to the previous scenario."

"Well, then, we got a guy. Let's go there and see what he says."

"What do you mean, you've got a guy? Does the family regularly subcontract out occult services?" James is keen to know the answer because it's piqued his interest and it's something he could potentially add to his portfolio.

"Like I say, we got a guy. We always go to him when we get weird stuff." James actually looks hurt at this, Paulie notices. "This kind of weird stuff, I mean. Aw, you thought you were the only number on the rolodex? Dream on. You're good, but as you said this ain't your area of expertise. Time we paid a visit to someone who might be able to give us an answer."

"So where are we going? To see a priest?"

Paulie laughs, a throaty rattle that sets James' teeth on edge. "Nah, he ain't no priest. He's a chef." Now James looks intrigued, impressed even.

Clearly the other experts on the books were as esoteric in their subject matters as he was.

"He'll be over in Hell's Kitchen." Paulie lights another cigarette, then realizes he has a passenger and makes the concession of rolling down the window, even though that fucks up the A/C. "I'm sure you'll get on just fine. We call him Frankie Pentangles."

***

James isn't sure what to expect when they finally arrive at Frankie's. Hell, he'd been expecting a priest at first, so anything he encounters now is going to reflect oddly on his initial hunch of what a guy who was the go-to occult expert for a mob family looked like. He isn't expecting something quite this chaotic, though. Chefs of his acquaintance - of which there were admittedly only three - keep a tidy kitchen, with every knife and cleaver in place and pristine work surfaces. What greets him when he and Paulie pass through the beaded curtain masquerading as a doorway at the end of a trash-ridden alley is exactly the opposite. The kitchen is a riot of color and growth. Strings of onions and garlic line the lintel over the curtain portal. Bottles of oil and vinegar, amongst other less savory sauces, adorn a multitude of tiny shelves which seem to have grown organically from the walls in accordance with Frankie's needs. There's only one working table surface, but it's solid white marble and big enough to take up most of the floorspace. It's covered with herbs, some of which look like they've arrived straight from the pages of the Voynich manuscript: James doesn't recognize their look or smell at all. Partially that's because there are three pans - no, cauldrons - bubbling away on the hobs, filling the kitchen with steam and the pungency of passata. Frankie is stirring these vigorously as he chants over them in Latin. James isn't sure what he's chanting, but he's pretty sure it's no prayer.

"Hey, Paulie!" Frankie looks up from his work and greets Paulie like an old friend, first wiping his hands on an apron, then using those same great meaty paws to grab both of Paulie's in an extended shake. That apron. which must be nearly as old as Frankie is, has the same well-worn appearance as Frankie's features. He looks comfortable in his own skin and boy is there a lot of that skin. Frankie towers over Paulie, but then most people do. What James notices first about Frankie is his girth - a huge pot belly leading up to at least three chins. Great jowls with wide open pores mark a friendly face, but Frankie's eyes tell a different story. James knows those eyes. What he's seen and done, he instantly assesses, is nothing to whatever Frankie has filled his days and nights with. So, despite initial appearances, James knows to take this guy seriously. He doesn't even ask about the occult symbols drawn on the other door to the kitchen. In any other circumstance James would assume those symbols were drawn in blood. Here, he's pretty sure it's spaghetti sauce. As they get talking, James realizes that to Frankie, they might as well be the same thing.

Paulie, evidently a frequent visitor to Frankie's kitchen, pours himself a large glass of red wine from a faded green bottle on the countertop next to the hob, sits down and pops a green olive in his mouth. James just stands there, a stranger in a strange land, not sure what to do with himself. Frankie carries on stirring as he and Paulie chat briefly in Italian. James gets restless, shuffles his feet and then bends over to lift up the hunger stone. The others make room for it on the table. They're just about to start looking at it when they're interrupted by two younger Italians who push their way through the beaded curtain. One of them is bleeding from the corner of his mouth, the other is holding his arm as if it's sprained. Frankie offers them both a glass of wine, which they take, and a vial of what smells like garlic puree, which they take with them. Then they leave and Frankie turns around to face James.

"Eastern European gangs brought in a vampire to help secure their territory. Ain't no working with those schmucks." He looks James up and down, gauging his reaction. James doesn't budge, but inside he's full of questions, which somehow Frankie picks up on.

"Yeah, vampires exist. Yeah, garlic works. It ain't some heavenly power, I'll leave that kind of blessing to a priest. It works because it comes from the same land as the vampire. That's sympathetic magic for you. That's how myths are made, sonny."

James looks down at the stone. "So, what do we have here?" He needs time to compartmentalize what was just said, to pick apart every detail before he can ask meaningful questions. And time may not be something that they have.

43

Frankie blows some of the dry summer dust from the top of the stone, then brushes it lightly with olive oil to clean it up. He does this with such reverence and in such silence that the only sounds in the kitchen are the sauce bubbling and Paulie's slurping. He takes a step back and wipes his brow.

"Well, this ain't good. Not good at all. Glad you brought this to my attention, Paulie." He shakes his big head, sending little puffs of flour into the air like dandruff. "The usual routines won't help so much, but I'll do what I can."

Paulie mutters a thanks while spitting out an olive pit. In the seconds of silence that follow, James realizes he's going to have to be the icebreaker.

"So, I judge from everything so far that this is designed to keep some kind of monster locked up? That monsters exist and you...err...you help fight them?" He's struggling now not to ask a thousand questions at once, so he focuses on just one more. "How do we put it back?"

The look Frankie gives Paulie says, 'where did you get this guy?' Then he turns back to James.

"Most people start off by asking what the usual routines are, you know."

"Except you just told me that the usual routines won't help much. So that's something that can wait. And believe me, I will ask that later."

Frankie nods again. "Well, this here is what you call a hunger stone, but not one that warns of a drought. It means that something's hunger needs to be satiated before it can rest again. And what this thing eats..." He runs a fat finger over the little

44

grooves full of oil on the stone, as if reading it again carefully, then looks up straight from his bloodshot, haggard eyes into James' unblinking ones. "What this thing eats is us."

James does blink though, just once, and pretends it's just from the smoke and heat of the day, and the city, and the kitchen. He's spooked, not because there are already dead people involved and may be more, but because he doesn't know yet how to fix this situation and that makes him uncomfortable.

"How many 'us' are we talking about?"

Even Paulie thinks this is cold and he's made more people dead than James has had hot dinners. Though as the conversation continues, that turns out to be not many hot dinners at all. He laughs nervously.

"That's why we call him Iceman, Frankie. Cool as a cucumber."

"It's already dried up at least three police officers. It may also have fed on Feds." This unintentional joke elicits a little chuckle from Paulie. "Plus, we never found all the body parts we were looking for. What I mean is, it may already be resting, and we should deal with it before it gets hungry again, or wall it in if it's already satiated."

Frankie lets out a long, drawn-out breath which is so garlicky James can smell it from the other side of the table. "You'll have to memorize those odd sigils around the edge of the Elder Sign - that's the little tree branch - and reproduce them on a second stone without your brain frying. What's more, you'll have to do that in situ. I'll mix up something that'll help. In the meantime, we'll need to mix

45

something else up that I ain't got in my kitchen. I assume that either or both of you gentlemen are familiar with a cement mixer."

Paulie makes a couple of calls to what he calls his cobbler, still sipping on the wine, which visibly irritates James. Frankie, who is pounding a mixture of garlic, dried oregano and fresh-cut basil in a giant pestle and mortar, looks to bust to interrupt. Occasionally, he mutters something over them, either in Latin or Italian but James isn't sure which.

"How is that helping?" It's not that James is exasperated, so the question doesn't come out like that - it's a genuine enquiry. He does wait until Frankie has finished though.

"It's magic."

James remains silent.

"OK, I'll go into a little more detail without giving away all the secrets. It works a little like the garlic does. It'll work on Paulie here because he grew up eating this. Cooking is alchemy, y'see. You follow a certain recipe, or sometimes you have a little experiment. Either way, it produces something of lasting value. I can turn pasta into gold, metaphorically, when I serve it up and people are nourished by it - and I don't just mean physically." Frankie wheezes a little, clearly exhausted by the physical and mental effort he was putting into this concoction. "All the little habits you learn - how to best cut up garlic, how to stir the sauce, they're like little rituals. They make the magic work. See?" He holds out a ladle for James to taste from, which he tentatively does. Frankie looks deep into him again,

46

eager to see the reaction. When there isn't one, he's disappointed.

"Where are your people from?" On the other side of the table, Paulie finishes his drink and laughs.

"He won't say. Part of his mystique." The tone is definitely mocking. James frowns.

"What do you usually cook for yourself?" Frankie tries a different tack. Here it is, James' first visible squirm. A question he doesn't want to answer, since he lives mostly off protein shakes, energy drinks and vitamin supplements.

"Look, Paulie there, he's fortified by that wine. That wine comes from the same part of the old country his family grew up in. These connections are important. Capice?"

James gets the idea. "I'm Scots Irish." That's what his name says, that's what he sticks to if pushed. He doesn't mention the Quebecois connection, since nobody knows his name is Devereux and that's how he wants it to stay.

"Well then, have a glass of whisky. It'll do wonders." Frankie goes to reach down to a battered white cabinet in the corner by the other door.

"I don't drink."

Both the Italians turn on him at that point. Paulie looks surprised, Frankie looks disappointed.

"Better piggy-back on our good fortune then." He opens a little cupboard above the drinks cabinet and withdraws a little cardboard box tied up with a silver ribbon. "It won't work as well, but it'll do something. Here." He thrusts the box into James' hand and sits back down.

47

"This thing in the tunnel is what the lore calls a flying polyp. It's invisible to the naked eye and you'd better pray you don't see it anyway. If you thought those symbols messed with your mind, you ain't seen nothing yet. Firearms will barely hurt it. You can electrocute it if you're lucky. But best just try and seal it back in with a new flagstone."

James opens the box to reveal four little tube-shaped shells of dough stuffed with cream. He looked up at Frankie.

"Those are the only shells you'll need in this fight. Trust me. Leave your gun. Take the cannoli."

They leave Frankie finishing off the last of the wine as Paulie chuckles all the way back to the car.

***

The heat hasn't diminished even though it's early evening by the time they get back to the reservoir. The stubborn sun has apparently hardly dipped an inch. They arrive at a scene that's evidently been disturbed since they were last there.

"Man, your car's been trashed." Paulie is trying not to laugh at James' misfortune, but his sick humor is tempered, mostly by the fact that James doesn't seem to care. There are heavy dents on the roof where it looks like something very heavy has landed and then sat for a while. The trunk has been utterly trashed, picked apart and left a wrangled, twisted mess of metal, the contents absent.

"Like a tin opener..." Paulie mutters, mostly to himself. He's scared now, probably more scared than he's been in his long, violent life and keeps looking up at the sky until he remembers that

Frankie said the thing's not visible to human eyes. Then he looks even more worried.

James is busy with the rest of the scene, working out what happened and what it can tell them about their foe. If he's annoyed at the damage to his car, scared at what they might be facing or has any feelings at all, he's not showing them beyond a certain tenseness in his shoulders. That in itself might just be battle-preparedness though. James' fight-or-flight reaction is even more heavily skewed in one direction than Paulie's.

Paulie's guys have evidently delivered the cement mixer and some supplies. It also appears they left in a hurry, as evidenced by the skid marks in the dry dirt at the edge of the car park, but there's no other sign of a struggle. James takes a few photos of the car on his phone, including a couple of close ups of the giant five-toed radial footprints on the roof. He's using this to assess the size and weight of the enemy, assessing what they might be facing even though he still hopes they won't need to face it. Then he turns his mind to the pressing practicalities of the situation.

"The cement's nearly ready. Help me pour it out into a decent sized slab." James is keenly aware of their environment and the tasks ahead of them - getting the slab down the side of the reservoir before it sets properly and then this weird ritual Frankie has primed them for. If he wasn't so focused on them then he'd be more worried that Paulie has lost some of spark and complies to his request without quips or complaint.

"Right, it's done. Now all we gotta do is get it down this pit, and quick. I don't wanna be no monster's dinner." Paulie actually heaves the slab up and carries it himself, carefully at the edges so as not to ruin the wet cement, which is already starting to set in the extreme heat. He's aware that James already seems to have his hands full. Two assault weapons crisscross his lean, muscled torso and there are a handful of grenades and a taser on his utility belt. Over his shoulder, James has a large bag though Paulie isn't sure what's in it, except that it doesn't look like people for a change.

They're about two-thirds of the way down when everything goes straight to hell. It starts with a strange disturbance in the air around them, like a heat haze suddenly descending on them both. It prickles their skin and makes their hair stand on end. Before they can react, there's a strange mixture of noises - a whistling of the wind, a whirring of metal blades clashing against each other, a low hum which seems to throb in the air around them. Then the winds pick up, throwing dust in their faces, scraping their skin with its heat and fury. Then there's a sudden shift in the air as the creature actually appears above them for a single moment. That moment is enough to drive both of these hardened men to utter panic, fear, and lunacy.

There are long, thin tendrils which emanate from what James presumes is the creature's head, though this proves difficult to determine as there are several mouths across the surface of the thing's thick gray hide and each of those slavering jaws are brim-filled with teeth sharper than Frankie's knives. Long barbs also protrude from that skin, except where its form tapers down to a resemblance of a tail, though that also ends in some sort of opening the purpose of which James is keen not to discover. What passes for eyes are softly glowing palpating growths around the principal mouth. James gets one good look at this before the dust storm blinds his vision and the sheer horror of what they face assaults his senses. He manages in that moment to reach down to his belt and grab a handgun, which he then proceeds to fire blindly, more in desperation than hope.

Paulie fares a little better. He raises the slab against his head, straining every muscle in his skinny body but protecting him from the worst of the dust storm and sparing him the bother of actually seeing the thing in the flesh. He continues to stagger down the side of the reservoir, hoping that James is either going to keep up or remain behind to deal with the creature. It doesn't immediately occur to him that James can presently do neither of those things. This immediate self-preservation saves him from the mental assault, but by marking himself out as the greater threat it does nothing to prevent him from the physical. The first swoop nearly knocks him off his feet. The thing is nearly four times Paulie's height and considerably bulkier. It uncoils in the air above him and dives straight down again. This time it hits home. Paulie, still managing to grip the slab he has to enchant at the entrance, is knocked over and tumbles down the side of the pit, leaving James on his own.

James recovers quickly, just in time to see Paulie's hasty, forced descent through the air as he struggles to slow his fall. His initial view of the creature was so brief and so deleterious to his concentration that he hasn't been able to identify any possible weakness in the thing's body. For the first time in his life, he's starting to regret the choice of tools he's brought with him. Not that he's ready to embrace Frankie's unorthodox approach, but he'll definitely consider it if he survives the day. There's a moment of respite when he realizes the thing's attention is elsewhere, then a moment of horror when it dawns on him that he'd better get its attention back, pronto, otherwise Paulie will have no chance with the slab. He unslings an assault rifle and gets to work.

Paulie is at the cliff bottom, His shirt and waistcoat are torn to shreds and there are broad lacerations down his back from where he's plunged down the scree, blood mingling with sweat in a hundred tiny wounds. He's covered in a thick layer of dust, disoriented and winded. Down but not out. He has a thumping headache, though that's more from the mental assault of the creature than the background problems of the heat, the dust, and the wounds. He fist-pumps the air to punctuate his moment of triumph. The slab is intact, the tiny jars of herbs and spices from Frankie are miraculously intact, for which he actually takes a moment to thank the saints. Then he orients himself and begins scrabbling around the bottom rim of the reservoir to get to the entrance of the hole. Above him, he can hear the familiar sound of gunfire. He knows from

Frankie that this isn't likely to do any good, but through the brain fog he knows that's not the point. James is putting his life on the line to buy him some time. He tries to spit out the dust in his mouth, but it's too dry to have any effect. Sitting down to get his breath, he opens one of Frankie's vials - which happens to contain a good Perricone - and takes a swig.

James curses and drops the spent gun, which clatters down the cliff. Taking a moment to locate Paulie, he looks down and spots him sitting on a rock drinking something like he's on a damn picnic. Maybe it's part of the plan, maybe Paulie's just a liability at this point. The thing is still up there, somewhere, in that cloud of dust. In fact, it's only because of the dust that he can see the outline of it. He reaches around into his backpack and struggles with a side pocket until the flap opens and he pulls out his night vision goggles. That ought to even the odds. Looking through them makes no difference though, there's still only a rough outline of where the thing actually is. He swears and leaves them dangling around his neck while he plans his next move. That's when the monstrosity lets out a great shriek which makes his eardrums bleed and dives, dives, dives. It's forgotten about him and gone back to Paulie.

Paulie is spent, breathless, bleeding but his head is no longer pounding. He stands right where the former stone was and has dropped the new one in place. It's quiet in here, and cool, and both of these things serve to calm him somewhat. His bloodied knuckles close in on a jar of pureed herbs which he pries open and then dips an olive branch in. Starting to recite the Latin phrases, fresh in his mind from Frankie's instruction, he thanks James for buying him some time with his life. As he starts chanting, part of him takes stock that despite his whole brain feeling like its melting from the inside out, he has become extraordinarily focused on the ritual. So much so that two things that should occur to him pass him by completely. Firstly, that with patterns swirling round in his vision, he wouldn't notice if the horror came up right behind him at the moment. Secondly, that what he's doing at the moment is effectively trapping the flying polyp outside the tunnel rather than inside. Only when he can see James in his peripheral vision, frantically waving his arms and shouting, does he realize either of these and by then he's so involved he can't stop.

James beckons at Paulie frantically, but to no avail. He can't see the monster, can't feel its presence at all and that worries him, but not as much as what Paulie's up to. How intelligent is that thing anyway? Does it realize that Paulie's about to accidentally grant it eternal freedom from its tunnel? Is that what it wants? He'd managed to get a tracker on it earlier with a lucky shot but even the screen output showing its location far above them is blurry and indistinct. He'll need to attract its attention again and somehow get it back inside the tunnel, past the both of them, without either of them getting hurt. None of the various mouths and tendrils and barbs and coils on the thing look like something he wants to get bitten, stung, or hit by. He's about to go back to the tunnel mouth when something comes crashing down on him. It's not the polyp, though. It's his car.

Paulie is lost in the moment, tracing arcane glyphs into the drying cement with an olive branch and chanting phrases he's only heard once before which nevertheless seem to exit his lips with perfect clarity. He's never felt such serenity before. It leaves him breathless. It leaves him vulnerable.

Only a few seconds after the car crashes in front of James' eyes, knocking him to the tunnel floor mere inches from Paulie, the air starts to vibrate again, and the thing slowly congeals into the air in front of him. James has only one close-up weapon, but he figures it could irritate the thing long enough to make him the primary target again. He whips out the taser and blasts it straight at one of the masses of eyes surrounding the central maw. There follows the most execrable screech he's ever heard, and all the tendrils whip around blindly. Three of them make contact with his bare arm and leave stinging welts on his flesh.

That got its attention.

Once it has stopped thrashing, it pulsates and writhes again, sending a hot blast of air and a wretched hollering whoop into the tunnel. James can't see it now, but he knows when it's getting close to him because he's used the one thing that he picked up at Frankie's which he figured might actually be of practical use. Even in the gloom of the tunnel, he can make out approaching five-toed prints in the flour he's strewn around the entrance. Waving a flare in one hand, he's pretty sure he's got its attention. It barrels past Paulie and heads straight at him.

"Si videries me lamentate." Paulie speaks the last words of the chant, the warning that will tell people not to disturb this place again. He's barely conscious now, not from any wounds but from the pressure on his mind and the disturbances in his peripheral vision which resemble the remnants of a really bad LSD trip. But he holds on long enough to draw the branch of the Elder Sign onto the slab. There's an unholy wail from deeper in the tunnel which he can just make out before he passes out. It's done.

James reaches Paulie only moments later. His arms aren't strong enough to lift him because the sting of the tendrils have done their work and he can't even lift his gun. But he can drag Paulie out to the sunlight. Those last few moments of that battle, where the thing manifested long enough to stare directly at him, all its eyes ablaze with millennia of blind rage and hatred, those moments just before he managed to slide beneath it and skid across the tunnel floor, will stay with him for a while, but for now there is only silence and the lingering heat of the setting sun.

They don't talk to each other at all on the way back. Paulie drops him off at a bar in Queens without even realizing where it is that James has asked to be dropped off. It's genuinely amazing that he managed to grip long and strong enough on the wheel to get them both back to the city.

***

James goes straight into the long, low, nearly empty bar, ignoring the few disapproving looks he gets at his appearance. When he finally stops shaking, he manages to clean himself up a little in the restroom and then stares at himself in the mirror for what seems like an eternity. Then he goes back into the bar and orders a whisky. His hand grasps the glass with the loose grip of the utterly unfamiliar as he raises it to his mouth in a solitary toast to success.

"It works, doesn't it?"

Frankie sits down next to him. James doesn't even know how he's got here, then remembers Paulie must have told him.

"It's starting to."

"Uh-huh."

"Tell me more. I want to know everything."

Brighton Baroque

A gull wheels across the sky at sunset, keen eyes surveying the surf. Unlike its compatriots, it is not seeking sustenance. This gull has a mission. It dips its ink-tipped wings and dives, dives, dives. Over the entrance to the chain pier, causing considerable consternation among the pedestrians populating the promenade. Over the Victoria fountain with its stone dolphins. It rests briefly on the lip of a balustrade on the Royal Pavilion, not so much as to get its bearings as to gather its thoughts. Will they remember the ancient compact? Will they honor it, as their mother and father would have wished? Will they be of suitable character and bearing to deal with the resurgent menace?

Scratching its beak against a wing - it is unused to such complicated thoughts and doesn't really want them - it flaps down to the Theatre Royal opposite and raps politely on a small window to the left of the stage door. Then it paces back and forth, pecking occasionally at the fine film of dust while it waits for a reply.

Beyond that window in a stuffy, undersized dressing room, two figures argue in raised but perfectly formed voices.

"Clementine, dear heart, please be sparing with the foundation. We haven't a lot left." The voice is clear, somewhat shrill in indignation, and loud enough to be heard in any of the dressing rooms, though not on the stage.

"Oh Clement, joy of my life, please do shut your perpetually whingeing cakehole and pass me my moustache." This voice is deeper, heartier somehow, but no less sonorous.

There is a knock at the door - fragile, unsure - and it opens slightly. A nervous figure enters with a tray.

"Champagne for you both. And chocolates." He indicates a small box stuffed with peppermint creams fashioned to resemble miniature seashells.

"Well, that's thoughtful. Isn't that thoughtful, sister of mine?"

The gull looks on nervously, trying to peek through the thick layer of grime. It hops back and forth for a few moments, making sure it has the right window, and taps again furiously. If these two are meant to save the day, then the day is in a lot of trouble. Not to mention tomorrow.

Finally, the window creaks open ever so slightly, enough for it to stick its head through and fully inspect the appointed saviours of the town. As it does, it is met with a shriek of horror which only a trained actor could muster.

"Shoo! Get away, wretched vermin!" A procession of objects, ever increasing in size and hardness, are catapulted in its direction. It dodges deftly, then re-alights on the sill and - in a welcome interlude to the harassment - scratches with its beak in the dirt.

"IT HAS RETURNED"

Both the humans in the room change their demeanor rapidly. They invite it inside, even prepare it a cushion, now they're aware what it is.

Not just a gull. A harbinger of ill omen. A message from beyond the grave, somehow - from their own dear father, departed sadly these 22 years. This is the day they were warned about. A day they have been preparing for. Just not one they had expected to interrupt their three-week star billing at the Theatre Royal.

"Clementine, sister dearest?"

"Yes, brother of mine?"

"It's time to get things started." Clementine was already removing some of the more obvious elements of her outfit - the top hat, the glue-on moustache, the outlandish monocle that gave her stage gentleman-persona that air of distinction.

Clement had a much longer job of it. He was still removing layers of crinoline, bustle and silk bloomers as his sister watched in what would have been taken for impatience had it not been punctuated with occasional mirthfulness. Finally, in a last act of exasperation, he clutched at his pearls and declared. "Oh, do help me, sister of mine. It's one thing to be seen in this on the stage, it's quite another to wear it on the street, let alone when we are about Society business!"

Clementine reached over, snatching her brother's hands together imperiously and commanding him to stand still while she disengaged him from masses of female undergarments. When she was done, Clement pecked her on the cheek by means of thanks.

"Where would I be without you? Now, where's our avian visitor gone?"

"He's behind you."

The two of them turned round together and regarded the gull with utmost seriousness.

"Can it talk, do you think?"

"Not so, brother dear, not so. It is a mere messenger. A warning that another threat from the sea has come. We must act swiftly to determine the nature of the menace. Are you ready to travel?"

"As good as I can be. Besides, nobody will really notice in the dark. We're bound to attract some attention, but we've carefully cultivated an air of eccentricity that will serve us well. Ready when you are!"

At that, they left their dressing room and made their way to the stage door, evading angry glances from both stagehands and their producer. The show must go on, but tonight it was a different show.

Back in the dressing room, the lone gull looked up wearily, grabbed one of the elegantly wrapped chocolate shells in its beak and flew back out of the window, high and away into the night air.

***

Clementine June Weatherlie and Clement August Weatherlie made their way from the stage door through the dingy alley at the back of the theatre and ran briskly across the road, lest they be recognized by the crowd outside the door who had come to see them perform. This managed, Clementine took a key from her reticule while her brother looked over his shoulder ready to fend off any autograph hunters. The key fitted perfectly into a little-known door in the grounds of the Pavilion, a door that had not seen much use since the death of their father in the great storm of 1850. They were entering the local archives of the Aletheian Society - masses of parchments, tomes, objets d'art and occult paraphernalia meticulously collected by the previous generations who had served in the Society - including their dear departed father - and equally meticulously catalogued and maintained by their erstwhile personages. While they had dealt with all manner of supernatural threats in their time, they had been ultimately preparing for what they called The Threat From The Sea (they both agreed it was worthy of capitalization) - the very threat that had caused the great storm and taken their father from them too soon.

"Father's notes are quite clear on this, as you are aware."

Clement nodded in reply. "It would do us good to have a last review of them, I think, before we execute the plan of action."

"Agreed. Please be so kind, brother dear, to pass me 'The Book of All The Ancient Customs' and father's notes."

Clement fumbled at the latch of a cabinet, his hands shaking slightly, and opened it to reveal a treasure of terrible tomes. He reached for a weighty volume which had the singular pleasure of its own shelf and looked at the catch, fashioned to resemble two dolphins chasing each other.

The book set firmly on the table, Clementine opened it with tremulous hands and wondrous eyes. Here was the prize of their collection: the tome which bore the ancient compact between the fisherfolk of the shore and the townsfolk who had arrived later. Two copies of this tome existed - one for each party - and it was a matter of some consternation that the twins did not know which copy they had or how their father - on behalf of the Society - had come to procure it.

The volume itself was old - as old as the town of Brighthelmston - and the hinged dolphins gave way creakily to reveal the text inside. The contents were familiar to the twins, who had pored over it a thousand times in preparation for this day: how the townsfolk and the fisherfolk had banded together to rid the ancient town of the first menace from the sea, carefully annotated illustrations of its malevolent form and how to defeat it when it rose again. Of central concern in the appendices to the tome penned by their father was the following passage about how the threat became manifest:

"There has always been perceived among those who dwell on the coast a danger from the ocean that those who live inland cannot understand, whether from onshore storm, flooding, or malevolent aquatic fauna. Periodically, unknown triggers bring forth what I am forced to conclude is a manifestation of the collected consciousness made flesh; an enemy that can be fought and, one must hope, vanquished. This has been so since the first stories of knuckers in waterholes and talk of dragons in Ethelward's Chronicles."

"So," muttered Clement, "Are we to be gallant knights-errant and slay the beast with weapons? Or are we going to be more like the cunning Jim Pulk and bake it a poison pie? I confess my skills at either are somewhat lacking."

"Wits, I think, win the day," replied Clementine, "At least that would be my preference. Also, given the cyclical nature of attack and defense that father noted, I suspect we will have to face that poison ourselves - though it what manner I find hard to deduce - and should thus be prepared."

"Oh, joys," quipped Clement. "Can it be a surfeit of champagne? At least then I can die happily."

"Hush! No talk of dying, please, brother dearest. I think we need to bring this matter to the attention of the third member of our little circle and see what he has to say."

Clement harrumphed. "He never seems to say anything of import. But lead on!"

"Well, let's be away then and see what wisdom he's in the mood to dispense today."

***

Namrik had technically been a member of the Aletheian Society for fifty-two years, which would have made him one of the Society's longest-serving members were he actually a human being. Instead - its consciousness being a result of a wishing lamp being accidentally soldered on to one of Charles Babbage's prototype computational contraptions - Namrik was forced to eke out a meagre existence as a fortune telling machine beneath the chain pier, a favorite among the weekend crowd but a pale imitation of an unfulfilled destiny. The twins had first been introduced to him by their parents when they were young; it was only in discussion with the elders of the Aletheian Society that Namrik's true

64

history had come to the fore. It remained a mystery to Clement why the Society placed more stock in this machine than the abilities of their human agents. It was less of a mystery to Clementine, who was currently wondering why Clement was only wearing one shoe.

Clement fumbled in his pocket for a shilling and inserted it wearily into the slot. Namrik sprang into life, the cogs and wheels clicking and computing as the automaton's piercing blue eyes searched for the image of who had deigned to disturb him. Some two minutes later, after a not inconsiderable amount of jerky hand-waving beneath ill-tailored silk sleeves, the machine spat out a token. Clement withdrew it from the machine and looked it over.

YOU WILL MEET A TALL DARK STRANGER

Clement sighed.

"Let me try," muttered Clementine. "Pass me a shilling, darling brother of mine." Namrik's eyes glowed blue momentarily - had they ever done that before? she wondered - and there followed a long period of silence interrupted only by a series of clacks and whirrs until, eventually, his wisdom spent, Namrik spat out a second token which she turned over in her hand. Upon it there were no words, merely a picture of a shell. For a moment, she was one of mind with her brother.

"I've seen that before!" Clement exclaimed, tugging on her sleeve. "Somewhere recently…"

"Oh, do think clearly!" Clementine held her brother's hands in hers as she implored him to remember.

"In the tome! Wait, no, in father's notes! It's an ammonite!"

"Of course! It's a facsimile of a fossil, not anything current. The architect Amon Wilds decorated buildings with them all over the city, as a play on his name. And he was father's chief suspect, he accused Wilds of using his architecture as a geomantic summoning grid writ large over the whole town! That must be what Namrik is trying to tell us!"

"Wilds must be dead by now though, surely?" Clementine resisted the urge to slap her sibling. They should both be aware by now that things didn't always stay dead. Especially after that incident on the promenade last summer. Luckily, he corrected himself with an 'Oh,' and then tailed off.

"He died in 1833, brother dear, suspiciously only a few days after the collapse of the Anthaeum. It was the architecture not the architect that father suspected."

Clement straightened himself. "Well, nothing a few blows with a pickaxe won't cure, then! We can smash those shells and be done in one night!".

"We will need that pickaxe, that's true. Also, maybe a shovel. Brother dear, we need to raise the dead."

***

"The trouble with the dead," Clement mused as he wiped sweat from his brow. "Is that they should stay dead." He paused for a moment, leaning on the pickaxe in the ill-lit graveyard on top of the hill. It was trivial enough to find the architect's grave - there was a bloody great ammonite on it - but digging it up was hard work, especially as Clementine had insisted he did the work alone while she 'kept vigil.'

They had made their way to the rear of the churchyard undisturbed - it was past midnight now, they thought. The only person they had seen in the vicinity was a tall man dressed in an impeccable dark blue suit and matching top hat, who seemed quite unaware of their presence and was content to stare intently into the night sky, softly calling, as they crept past.

Now though, as she stood shivering, Clementine became acutely aware that they were being watched - by someone or something - and it gave her chills beyond that of a dark summer's night.

"Are you done yet?" She inquired over her shoulder.

Clement grunted in reply.

Then it came. A pair of glowing green eyes, descending at them from the heavens, and with it a vicious looking beak and long, white wings locked in a silent swoop.

"Aagh! Get away!"

Alerted by his sister's cry, Clement wasted no time in scrabbling from the half-dug grave to stand next to her, pickaxe at the ready, as Clementine removed a talisman from her reticule and flashed it before them in a series of rapid movements.

The gull dove again, but this time appeared to bounce off an impenetrable, invisible barrier and waddled away, stunned, and reeling.

"I say! That was a rather good trick!"

"It only works once. Quick, let us find some cover."

"They're not normally that vicious!"

"Yes, they are! What they aren't - normally - is nocturnal. Or possessed." Clementine ducked behind a tomb as the gull took off.

"Oh." Clement flailed at it with the pickaxe as it dived toward him.

"We need to get out of here, something is very wrong..."

"You're telling me! Possessed seagulls!? Whatever next!"

"Possessed actors? That's the same seagull that warned us in our dressing room." She dived behind a tombstone as the screeching began again. The gull wheeled in an arc across the night sky, biding its time.

"Huh?"

"The ammonite shape, we've seen that before."

"I know, it's..."

"Not in father's notes! In the dressing room. It's the same shape as the chocolates that were delivered to us."

Clement tripped and sank to his muddied knees; Clementine swung back and helped him up.

"The gull has parts of the green wrapper stuck on its beak."

Clement looked aghast. "I confess I didn't look that closely..."

"Run! Now!"

The two of them leapt out of cover and high-tailed it into what they hoped was the relative protection of the church. Momentarily safe, they gasped to recover both their breath and their wits.

"So, you think the chocolates were poisoned?"

"I believe them to be part of Namrik's warning. As dangers from the sea go, though…" Clementine peered out from under the porch toward the sky. "I'll take a gull over a shark. But we need to get back, first to the theatre to inspect the chocolates and then back to the archives for their safekeeping."

"You don't think the cast have…" Clement tailed off.

"Think, o joy of my existence, when was the last time you helped yourself to something unattended in a dressing room?"

"Oh Lord! We must make all haste!"

"Exactly."

The twins made short work of the journey back to the theatre, but the scene that greeted them was not what they expected. Entering through the stage door, ever alert, they had expected to encounter an entire cast of show-stopping actors with glowing eyes of emerald green. What they found instead, daubed on the walls in blue paint, was a series of glyphs that rendered them insensible. Both succumbed to the mind-numbing drowsiness the graffiti induced in them, collapsing first to their knees and then giving in to the oblivion of sleep. Whatever had chosen to menace them this night, it would appear its tactics had changed.

***

Silence. Near darkness. Only a dim twinkling from overhead, a reflection from the moon outside through layers of expensive glass.

69

Struggling with her bonds, Clementine called out to her brother.

"Clement, are you there?"

"Present, sister dearest."

"Where the Dickens are we, do you imagine?"

"We're in the Regent's Saloon, inside the Pavilion."

Clementine looked over, quizzically.

"I recognize the outline of the chandelier and this particular carpet stain."

Quite how her brother was intimately familiar with the interior decor of the ballroom could wait for another day.

"Help me out, would you? I can just about reach my knife if you loosen my rope a little…"

"Enough." A booming voice echoed throughout the room, quelling all attempts at escape.

"You will answer for your crime."

"Pray, what crime might that be?" Clementine replied sweetly, with only a tiny hint of sarcasm. "And while we're on the subject, since when do trials take place in the dead of night in formerly royal apartments?"

"Since Queen Victoria was persuaded to relinquish the Pavilion to us, The Society of Twelve."

Clementine hadn't actually been expecting an answer; but if she had, this was the answer she would have wanted.

"Free us and show yourselves! I believe we can come to an accord against the return of true evil to our beloved town. I say to you now, whose sacred

70

societal name is known to me, that we are not your enemies."

There followed a series of hushed, frenzied whispers and the same voice spoke.

"Very well. We will show ourselves."

A flickering of light; the flare of a lantern. Then, the Society revealed their true forms to the horror of their still-bound prisoners.

***

Had Clementine still been wearing her monocle, it would at this point have fallen comically from her face at the sight before them.

She looked over at her brother. Clement, for his part, was clutching his fist in his mouth in a semblance of fear. Though it was just possible, she thought, that he was doing it to stifle a giggle.

"We are, as you can see, naturists."

One must assume that the sight of the twelve society members in their altogether was used predominantly as a shock tactic. On this occasion, it had been found wanting. There was an awkward pause measured only by the uncomfortable shuffling of feet. Clementine, who had seen more semi- or unclothed persons in her theatrical career than she cared to think about, merely blinked, and then retorted.

"And we, as you can see, are cross-dressing thespian twins. We are also the representatives of the Aletheian Society in Brighton, sworn by sacred duty to protect the realm of her majesty from supernatural incursions and malignant otherworldly artefacts."

71

"The Leafy Urn Society?" The same voice boomed, but with a mouth behind it this time; a mouth attached to a face and a naked body which was somehow glowing now with its own cerulean light. "Never heard of you."

"What gives you the right to hold secret court over our fates?" This new outburst came from Clement, still struggling with the ropes. "From what sacristy do you proclaim dominion over the unseen and unworldly, as we do?"

"By ancient compact, we protect this town from monstrous incursions from the ocean," the voice intoned. Clementine could make out more of the form attached to that voice now as it shuffled slowly forward. A thin, translucent man, but a man, nonetheless. He trailed behind him some contraption which seemed to be affixed to the rear of his neck and upper arms by lengths of translucent tubing, through which ran a clear liquid. What fresh madness was this?

"Inter Undes et Colles Floremus." The intonation echoed through the superb acoustics of the Regent's Saloon.

"What's he saying?" Clement was frantic now. "What's he SUMMONING?" He was nearly free of the ropes with all the frenzied struggling, but his sister had stayed unflinching, still bound.

"Hush, brother dearest. That's the town motto."

"By the Book Of All The Ancient Customs of the Toune of Brighthelmston, we are bound to protect the coast from the dangers of the sea."

Clementine wasn't going to question where he'd produced the book from. There were some things that were best left unquestioned. As he drew closer, his full visage became visible by the lantern light and its own eerie inner glow; gaunt, haggard, and speckled with liver spots, the vestige of a grey beard trailing to his neck; beneath it, barely visible, a recognizable form in amber at his throat. An ammonite.

For the first time in this sorry affair, Clementine gasped.

"You're him! You're Amon Wilds!"

"Indeed, young woman. And I am, as you can see, neither dead nor buried."

Clement, who had wrestled free from bondage at last, rose and turned to look at the ancient man now all but hunched over his sister. Whatever he was about to do, he had better do it quickly. As Wilds raised the book in his hand, however, he found himself commenting rather than confronting.

"Oh! The Book of Customs! We have one of those in the basement, don't we, Clementine my heart?"

Clementine sighed. All their cards were revealed, all the tension had left the situation. The other eleven members were at first intensely shocked at this news, then mollified.

"If that is so, then you are the partners we hoped for." Wilds spoke for them all. "Let us speak further."

***

"Father was convinced it was you." They had all settled in now like old friends, taking sips in Fitzherbert's after hours. "Said the ammonites gave

73

you away. The exact form that was needed to summon creatures from the depths."

"Such an object, once used for one purpose, can be more easily diverted to the opposite. The ammonite architecture protects us all now - to some extent - by the principles of sacred geometry. Safe enough for most of us, but not her royal personage, which is why she was advised to vacate the Pavilion and leave the building to us." He added a brief afterthought. "And I keep myself alive, as it were, by having the life-giving seawaters of Brighton running through my veins rather than blood."

"How is it you have a copy of our book?" interjected Clement, sour at being left out of the discussion.

"When the customs were first scribed down, two copies were made. One remained in the town in a chest secured by three locks, which has been guarded by the Dippers on behalf of the Twelve ever since. We did not know what happened to the other."

"Somehow it either fell into father's hands and he was recruited by the Aletheian Society, or he was already a member and procured it," finished Clementine, quaffing back another tot of gin. "We may never know..."

"You must return it to the fisherfolk in the morning. That much is imperative. We will take care of your cast until the work is done. I'm sure it won't be the first time some of them have spent the night in the cells." Wilds was thoughtful. "Do you think our plan will work? Are you prepared to enact it?"

74

"We will need to rest first. But yes, we'll do it."

"Then we will see you there, in Pool Valley, to lend our aid."

It had not escaped the twins' notice that this was exactly where their father had died.

***

Dawn is a taxing time of day; more so when one has only had three hours sleep at most. Clement rubbed his eyes and groaned, standing behind his sister on the mist-laden beach, chill with morning air.

Clementine stood in conversation with three fishermen, pipes lit and arms folded. She repeated the words Wilds had taught her to say. "By ancient compact, we claim our rights to one twelfth of all your sardines." Eyebrows were raised, and one among them stepped forward.

"You are new. You are from them?"

"We are from … another … its complicated. We're working with them, but we are also the ones in possession of your tome." She snapped her fingers and Clement moved forward at the cue, nearly tripping on the unstable shingle. He handed it over. They spoke among themselves for a few moments in a strange cant Clementine couldn't make out.

"It's back. We have a plan to take it out, but we need your consent and your control over the tome to be restored." Clementine took the initiative in the dialogue, as she usually did, before her brother began tripping over his own words.

"And a few fishing nets would be good, maybe a harpoon or two." Clement was impatient, shivering.

75

"Aye, we've sensed its approach. Storm clouds have been gathering for days. Do we go now?"

"Just to Pool Valley. We can use its unique position as the underground confluence of the Wellesbourne and the Westerbourne streams to imprison its physical form, but it won't go easily." Clementine had been impressed with the scale of Wilds' plan. From the Aquarium to the new Goldstone pumping station, it seemed that all the recent construction in Brighton had been designed for this specific purpose.

The fisherman nodded, then turned and shouted to the others who were busy preparing their nets. Clement stood alongside his sister; his neck crooked as he eavesdropped on whatever it was the fisherfolk now began saying amongst each other in their strange shared language.

"They've agreed to it then! Good." Clementine turned, quizzically.

"You understand their cant? Brother dear, you do amaze me!"

"Sister of mine, that is Polari. It's used by fishmongers and queens both. I can understand every word of it. Shall we go?"

The twins walked grimly, hand in hand, to the place of confrontation, trailed by a dozen hardy fisherfolk with a host of barbed weapons.

***

Whatever they had expected at Pool Valley, it certainly wasn't nothing. In the dim glow of the dawn, the twins and their allies surveyed the scene. No storm, no flooding, no menace. One of the shops

76

was open, however, which was certainly strange at this time. Clement nudged his sister.

"'Edmunds Chocolates.' Must be the place." As if at their bidding, a thin frame appeared at the doorway, human but barely so, eyes lit with a blazing emerald green. One harpoon flew over their head and clattered harmlessly to the floor at its feet. Enraged, it let out an unearthly screech and dropped to all fours.

"Now!" shouted Clement. Two of the Society of Twelve, marked as their 'Dipper' guards by their elegant bathing costumes, struggled with the manholes to the drains as the fishers began to encircle the enemy.

It grew in size, audibly popping joints and letting out howls as it did so. Clouds began to gather overhead, blotting out the sun, and then it started to rain. The scaled monstrosity that now gibbered and writhed before them struck out with a savage claw, rending one brave fisherman in half.

"Westerbourne, now!" Clementine roared the order, struggling now to be heard above the torrential rain. There was a great clunk and the drain gushed forth its load; fresh water to add to the rain. The creature hesitated slightly, spinning its slavering jaws in torment.

"Wellesbourne!" The second drain opened, the swell of the Wellesbourne spreading from the drain at the opposite side of the courtyard.

"Clementine! It's working!" Wilds, surveying from above, shouted. "But it's not enough! Dam the coastal barrage, that will divert the flows! Both water sources must be in full flow for the scheme to have effect!"

The twins cursed as the creature shrugged off attack after attack. The water was ankle deep now as they sloshed their way toward the promenade, deftly avoiding tooth and claw alike in their struggle. The Twelve had nearly finished the barrage, just a few sandbags left...

The draconic form writhed and twisted, held down now by nets, and constrained by the fresh water flushing the poison from its mind and body. It lashed furiously over and over again, gibbering, howling, the light dying within it until it was no more than a shell of itself.

Clementine paused for a breath. "It's done."

Wilds approached, dragging his brine tank behind him. "It is over. We can take it from here. We thank the Aletheian Society for its valuable assistance."

Clementine nodded. "If you ever need us again, you know where we are. Although don't try and enter without permission. There will be consequences."

"I might say the same of us. Still, there is no reason not to be cordial."

"Quite." Clementine turned to her brother. "We're on stage in three hours. Ready for it?"

"After this?" grinned Clement. "Child's play!" He sauntered off toward the Pavilion loudly singing a bawdy ditty. Clementine, with a sigh and a smile, followed him.

The Quiet Ones

"Five more last night." Arlette's voice was tired, scratchy. Jacques looked up from his patient in concern, not just for Arlette's voice but for the voices of so many others.

"That brings us to twenty-two." Jacques' broad shoulders slumped momentarily. He'd been up for thirty hours straight now. He knew he had to get some rest. He also knew that rest wouldn't come. Not until he had an answer.

"How can twenty-two people suddenly lose their voice?" Arlette's query was spattered with a light raspy cough and muted by the handkerchief she held over her mouth as she spoke. "What do you think, doctor?"

"I don't know. It's possible there's a natural explanation. I'm not entirely convinced until I do some more tests."

Arlette narrowed her brow and turned her head away slightly. She'd been working with Jacques at the Hope Springs Mission for a couple of months now and thought she had the feel of the man. He rarely spoke and even when he did, there was much he didn't say. She'd come to understand that what he didn't say was just as important as what he did. If he wasn't convinced there was a natural explanation for a sudden outbreak of what might well be laryngitis, then that meant he thought

79

something else was at work. Namely, a supernatural element. That made it her territory, not his.

"I'll ask around. See what people know. At least, the part that they're willing to say."

Jacques nodded wearily. At this rate there wouldn't be anyone left who could say anything, willingly or otherwise. There were few enough people in this forsaken place as it was. Most of those were troubled and traumatized. Perhaps that's what had drawn him here in the first place. From a young age, he had wanted to be a doctor. No, scratch that, what he had really wanted to be was a healer. There was a subtle difference in those words. He wanted to make people better, make the world a better place. It seemed fitting that the world had responded by putting him in a place where people really needed him. He stifled a yawn and walked over to the sink to wash his hands.

***

Arlette stepped outside the mission and looked down the street. At one end was the edge of town, where the road petered out into abandoned fields full of rotting corn stretched across the valley floor. She had thought about treading that road many times. Of getting out, like so many did. Somehow, she never managed to take that first step. There always seemed to be something drawing her back in. Behind the mission was the remains of what she once understood to be the lake, the crater caked now in a red-brown sludge of mud and rust. Even the spring which had given the mission its name had dried up. It was as if even fresh water - hell, anything fresh, wanted nothing to do with the eternal seeping entropy and decay which inculcated itself into every sinew, every fiber of one's being if one had been here long enough.

Arlette had been here three years.

In the other direction lay the mass of squalid shanties which separated them from what she liked to call the heart of darkness - the largely abandoned town center where the buildings were tall enough to cast long shadows over the rest of the town and where people rarely ventured these days. Everything salvageable or stealable had already been taken years ago. There was little left to loot. Arlette set off toward those shanties, past the boarded-up gas station and across alleys strewn with broken glass and equally broken lives. She knew who she'd approach first to try and get an answer. She only hoped she'd get there in time.

***

When he'd first rolled up here, the name of the mission caused Jacques to break out in a rare wry smile. There were no springs here anymore where the mountain had once given up its waters in torrents to feed the lake below. He knew enough geology to understand where those falls must once have been, how majestic they must once have looked. Once he'd gone inside the dilapidated building and found it empty, he also understood there wasn't much hope either.

What there was, still, was a mission. Not capitalized as it was on the creaking sign which hung half-heartedly outside the place, but the mission he'd felt a calling to all his life. He'd tried to leave his own demons behind when he'd left

Canada, but they had followed him incessantly, hounding his every move. Very well, he decided. Time to pick a battleground and meet them head on. Within days, he'd managed to salvage a few essential medical supplies. One day later, he had his first patient. Three days later on, that patient had become a conspirator against the darkness in his own life, just as he had in hers. When Arlette had first walked into the mission, her arms had been crisscrossed with bloody scratches so much that he'd feared a serious infection. Even then, she'd refused to say what had caused them. She hadn't needed to. As their eyes met in a flash of understanding, he knew they were somehow self-inflicted. He'd eventually teased an answer out of her, but that answer had come with additional questions. Fearful dreams, dark thoughts. Long screams in the night borne of a pain she carried inside which she felt compelled to make manifest on her body as she struggled against what she'd found here.

"Here be monsters." She had pointed toward the town as they sat outside the mission. "And here," she admitted, pointing to her head. "And here," pointing to his. Jacques merely nodded and they'd watch the sun go down and darkness fall, hand in hand, then arm in arm.

A lot had happened since then. Jacques didn't really understand what Arlette meant about the darkness in the heart of town. He'd assumed she was talking metaphorically. Now, he was sure she wasn't.

He had two patients with severe burns and no more painkillers. And twenty-two patients with what looked like laryngitis but wasn't. There was no cough, no splutter. What he could see when they tried to speak wasn't the exhaustion of someone with an illness, it was the exasperation of someone who can't express anything but fear, confusion, and anger.

Jacques had had some success with calming them down, getting them to write what they needed on paper. There were a few problems here though. It seemed that the neighborhood hadn't attracted a literate crowd. Hardly surprising. Many of his patients struggled to read and write at the best of times, but when they were in this state, they found it even more difficult to articulate. To top it all, the paper got moldy quickly. Ink dried up at an alarming rate. Pencil leads broke almost every time they were used. It was frustrating.

Currently, he was encountering that frustration first-hand in the person of Davey Winters who didn't need a larynx or a pen to tell Jacques just what he thought of him. Not when he had two huge fists to do the talking for him.

***

Arlette, meanwhile, had stopped to catch her breath at a dime store a few blocks over. Here, Sara was busy setting out the stalls outside and swatting off the bluebottles that had begun to buzz around angrily. She did this every morning with a blend of defiance and precision which Arlette found comforting. Sara was the only person Arlette knew who'd been here longer than her, which as far as she knew made her the longest-standing resident of Prosperity. Sometimes, Arlette wondered what kept her here. Deep down though, she knew the answer. Like so many others, Sara simply had nowhere else to go.

She looked over at the display of goods Sara had available. The usual array of scavenged parts, the few unlabeled tins of presumably-food. Arlette had bought one of those tins once and it had turned out to be rice pudding. She wasn't a fan, but had eaten it anyway, straight from the tin with a little spoon she kept in a makeshift pocket which was little more than a tear in the lining of her fleece.

"Hi Sara. How's things?"

Sara smiled and waved Arlette closer. She was normally more talkative than this. Unless...

Damn it all. You were my last chance.

Sara pointed at her throat and shrugged as Arlette swore quietly under her breath.

"You wanna come down to the mission and let Jacques have a look at it?"

Sara shook her head, her dreadlocks whipping animatedly as she did.

"Ain't no point," she seemed to say. After a protracted series of points and gestures, Arlette understood. "We both know that what's doing this ain't something he can fix."

"You got any ideas?" Sara saw and heard a lot as she scavenged her way through the city. Things that might be crucial to understanding how to deal with this. Or at least understand where it was coming from.

Sara shook her head again, then appeared to change her mind. She beckoned Arlette inside the shop. Arlette followed, knowing that if nothing else there would be good coffee.

***

Jacques managed to dodge the first blow but succumbed to the next two. Say what you like about Davey, but he still had a good right hook. Both their faces were contorted now, Davey's with rage and Jacques' with pain. Fumbling in a pocket, Jacques staggered backwards and managed to steady himself momentarily on the edge of a nearby cot before the flurry of Davey's blows became almost too much to bear. One punch sent him reeling across the floor, arms raised over his face in defense, giving him a few precious moments to extract the syringe from his pocket. Now all he had to do was get in close enough to use it without causing any further harm to either of them. As Davey loomed over him, red-faced and panting, Jacques thought he saw his chance and reached up, grabbing hold of the thin cotton of Davey's bloodstained shirt and dragging him down on top of him. When he went to administer the sedative, though, Davey countered with a jarring headbutt which knocked it out of his hand. The pair of them rolled around on the floor for what seemed like an age, neither of them landing any blows, just trying to disentangle themselves from each other. Davey grabbed him in a choke hold, threatening to draw out the last of Jacques' breath just as his own had been cruelly stolen from him. He was about to pass out when he felt Davey suddenly go limp on top of him, drool forming at the corner of his mouth. As he rolled the unconscious Davey off him, there stood a smiling Arlette, syringe in hand. His savior.

***

"Sara's lost her voice too."

They'd managed to pick up Davey between them and deposit his body unceremoniously on a makeshift bed. He'd recover soon enough, but they'd have some time to deal with the root cause. Jacques just hoped that time would be enough.

"I can't imagine Sara ever being quiet." Jacques winced as Arlette applied a cloth to his head wound.

"I know what you mean. Still, she showed me something on the map. She's seen something over at the old civic center. Here, look, she gave us an artist's impression." Arlette unfolded a sheet of paper and showed it to Jacques. It looked like the after-impression of a Rorschach test, all blotchy interlocking circles in shades of gray. Jacques wasn't sure whether to be impressed at the artist's hand he didn't know Sara had or to recoil in abject horror that this arrangement of muted, faded shapes might be something which had a physical presence in the town he'd come to call home.

Arlette watched him chew this over in his mind as she passed him a dented Styrofoam cup of coffee she'd brought back from the shop for her.

"Here, soldier, reckon you'll need this."

"Thanks." Jacques downed it on one, desperate to be more alert if not more refreshed. He winced.

"It's not that bad!" Arlette's gentle jibe woke him more than the coffee had.

"It's awful!"

86

"I guess you just get used to it. It's the best we got."

They both paused.

"You're going over, aren't you?"

Another pause, longer this time.

"We. We're going over. I'm not doing this alone; I'll need you there with me. Whatever it is, we'll deal with it. Besides, do you want to be here when Davey comes round?"

Jacques groaned.

"Thought not. We'd best get a move on if we're going to get there and back before dark."

It seemed he had little choice in the matter.

***

"Why do you do it?"

They'd reached the three-story civic hall and paused while they looked for the best way inside. The main doors stood impressively intact in their off-white marble with Greek columns on either side, laced with little cracks that had taken their toll over the years but still standing tall. Above them, a clock hung over the main entrance. It had long been abandoned by its hands and numbers. Just another faceless entity in the town, a reminder of what grandeur had lived here once.

"Why do I do what?" Jacques knew what Arlette meant. They'd had this conversation before, many times.

"Help people." Arlette spat in the road, her phlegm thick with the strong, black, awful coffee.

"You know why. They need it."

"OK, so why don't you help yourself while you're at it? Physician, heal thyself, right?"

"I can't. At least, not like that."

Arlette decided to change tack.

"Need to heal everyone else first, right? Like you're the Fisher King?"

"Well, this is certainly the Wasteland." Jacques managed a laugh, then retorted. "Why do you do it?"

"Why do I do what?" Arlette was enjoying the circular conversation.

"Keep looking. Investigating. What do you hope to find?"

"What makes you so sure there's something there to find? Ready to believe in the supernatural finally, man of science?"

"Spare me your jabs of mockery!" Jacques laughed again, but his face became serious. "I'm ready, I think. This place…" He didn't need to say any more. As if in response, what sun managed to permeate the low hanging mist had firmly retreated behind a looming array of murky gray clouds.

"Right on cue." That's what Arlette intended to say, but it came out differently. What she actually said was "……"

Jacques looked up, wide awake now. "Arlette?"

Arlette was frantically trying to indicate something to him, but he wasn't sure what. He thought - out of the corner of his eye - that he saw the tiniest shadow escape from the corner of her mouth and zigzag its way to the marble doors, only to get lost in the rest of the shadows. Surely a trick of the light? No, he said to himself. He had to be ready to believe.

First, though, he had another patient to deal with.

Arlette had collapsed to the ground in one of her frequent coughing fits but managed to recover quickly enough and shot him a scathing look which he interpreted as "Are you ready now?" She then produced two flashlights from her fleece and handed one to him. He rolled it over in his hand and tested it by twisting the end. It flickered briefly but shone well enough. Arlette had done the same.

They both nodded to each other and climbed the stairs to the marble doors. They didn't need words to understand each other's intentions. Not anymore.

***

It took their combined strength to lever the door open even a fraction, but that was enough to let them in. They looked around, flashlights gleaming paths. In the mist-choke darkness, these little paths of light showed long-forgotten pews, signs and documents. Whatever order might once have held sway here, it had long departed and left in its wake a ramble of rubble, all discarded bureaucracy of former lives. Human beings were not meant to enter these doors, not anymore. No sun or moon entered here. Nothing did any more. The central hall was silent as the grave but so much worse. The grave, after all, holds either the promise of finality or the chance of another life, a better life, an afterlife. There was no such hope here.

Arlette threw a pebble at Jacques to attract his attention. He was shivering in the sudden cold, standing there open-mouthed.

Snap out of it.

Jacques tried to speak. Tried to articulate what it was he was looking at. To put it into words. All that came to mind was all the voices from his past which had wounded him. His abusive father. Angry patients. An angrier girlfriend. They all told him the same. He was never going to amount to anything. He was useless. He was wrong. He was a waste of space.

All the voices said that, except one. Somewhere, somehow, amidst the sound and fury, one voice rang clear. It was Arlette's.

"Believe!"

And he did. Not just in the amorphous, slowly circling shapes which seemed to be edging forward towards him. Not just in the supernatural and otherworldly explanations which his rational mind had always wanted to dismiss.

For the first time in ages. Jacques believed in himself.

It was an absolute rush. He screamed out loud, all the repressed fury and rage and guilt within him came out in one long breath as he reached up to wipe the tears away from his eyes.

The form stopped moving.

He screamed again - louder than before - and Arlette's voice joined him, camaraderie in cacophony. Hundreds of voices then flitted between them, every soul silenced now released in a bitter, primal scream with only one message to convey. "Enough," it said. Not as a plea, but as a rallying cry. "Enough."

The monstrous form shifted in the shadows, turned, and gave flight. Jacques fell to the floor exhausted, and Arlene collapsed again, gasping with newly found breath. It would appear that for the time being that they had won out.

The darkness would come again, as it always did. But neither Jacques nor Arlette were willing to go gentle into that good night. Not while there was still hope, or while there was still a mission.

God Rest Ye, Merry

Meredith stood at the gates of Newfield Lodge, transfixed by the view through the flurry of snow which peppered the pathway to the great house itself. At her feet lay her paisley patterned holdall, bulging at what seams remained with all the trappings she thought she would need for the Christmas weekend. The holdall had seen better days, but not so Meredith. Though her face was flush with the cold, her body remained as limber as it had been in her youth when she had lived here.

The lodge had seen better days too, she thought. Whilst there had evidently been some efforts made to maintain the garden and keep the undergrowth from encroaching on the driveway, she could tell from this distance that the house itself had aged in those intervening years. Even through the light snowfall and the great gasps of misty breath issuing from her into the chilly evening air, she could spot a chimney high above that needed pointing, three boarded up windows and the overgrown curve of the path which led behind the facade of the lodge proper to access what they had always called the east wing.

They had always referred to it as the east wing, she realized, even though it was neither a wing of the lodge - having an entirely separate entrance hidden from the view of visitors by a grove of elm - or indeed located to the east. Its westbound entrance meant it got very little light early in the morning which ensured that the servants it once housed had to rely on a series of gongs and bells to awaken from their slumber and begin preparations to serve the family. And what preparations there were - work began early in the kitchen and the scullery for breakfast, with cook often choosing to sleep in the kitchen itself to keep the fires burning low overnight, While the family began their daily activities, an army of scullery maids, butlers, cooks, cleaning dailies, valets, maids and household managers went about their business silent and invisible to them.

She wondered idly if the old man would be there. Surely, he must have passed on by now, though she had heard no gossip to that end. A chill passed through her as she contemplated that. She couldn't recall any pleasant memories of the esteemed patriarch's near-tyrannical rule of the place. Most of the family avoided him whenever possible and many of the staff did likewise.

But they had enjoyed themselves here, she remembered with a smile. Yes, there had been good times between the wars when the place would often throng with weekend parties. Good times indeed.

Breathing on her hands to warm up - she had somehow neglected her gloves in packing - Meredith began to crunch her way down the driveway, lost in thought. So lost in fact that it almost came as a surprise to her when she stood before the imposing double doors, still formidable in their polished oak with the iron clasps only showing a few signs of rust. Here and there on the steps up there were a few flecks of snow and ice but it was clear someone else was already here and had thoughtfully swept aside what had managed to accumulate on the cold grey flagstones so as not to inconvenience the guests.

What guests though? Meredith had been surprised to receive an invitation to spend the weekend at the old place - at Christmas of all times! It had been many years since she'd set foot here or heard from anyone else. While she maintained to herself that it was curiosity which compelled her to reply in the positive, she also had to contend with the fact that it was really loneliness that had been the overriding imperative. Had she other invitations to spend the holidays, she might have forsaken this one in favour of a less bothersome journey.

Still, old acquaintances awaited within, presumably. There were no other footprints in the snow on the drive, she had noticed, and no sign of any vehicles. She wondered idly who, then, had swept the stair. Maybe some of the old staff still worked here, kept the place going? Interesting.

Smiling to herself as if she had discovered some important clue (Meredith often imagined herself as some dedicated lady sleuth laying bare the iniquities of ne'er-do-wells throughout the English countryside), she tentatively reached forward to ring the bellpull, only to find the door already slightly ajar. As if uttering a last gasp, the hinges groaned as she pushed, just as a gust caught her unawares from behind as if to hurry her inside.

Behind her, beyond the hedge and unseen even by her keen eyes, a figure stood, solid and silent, watching her as the door closed behind her and she finally entered the lodge proper.

***

Meredith emerged from the atrium into the great hall and deposited the heavy holdall at the foot of the stairway. She looked up at its great spiral through three floors of splendour, still bedecked with portraiture of the estate lineage, moustachioed and bearded all, their piercing eyes seeming to judge her as she shook the powder from her coat and laid it to rest on an ancient teak side table easily as old as the old pile itself.

The hall retained none of its warmth, being largely a cold and draughty room through which people passed rather than dwelt. Someone had been busy making it look festive though - a great fir stood tall at the north end, bedecked in homemade decorations of the kind they had fashioned themselves when young. A great wreath of holly and ivy took pride of place in the little table in the middle of the hall, so much so that even though it was propped up by a little stand it looked like it was about to lurch forward unexpectedly and hurtle pell-mell to the chessboard marble of the floor.

The stairs themselves had been decorated with strings of hellebore, their pastel pinks speckled with violet. They gave off a sweet, welcoming fragrance which made a firm change from the damp earth in the grounds. Meredith leaned forward to inhale deeper.

"Winter rose."

95

Meredith nearly tumbled forward and lost her balance, steadying herself on the banister rail only at the last moment.

"Sorry! A mop of unruly brown hair emerged from a door frame deep in one of the hall recesses. "Didn't mean to give you a fright."

"Well, a fright is what you gave me, meant or otherwise." Meredith rallied herself and turned to look at the approaching figure, clad as it was in a plain white shirt unbuttoned at the top and casual slacks spotted with white powder. She struggled momentarily to recall, as if a veil still stood between the years spent her in the past and her present incursion into those memories which floated around her like elusive ghosts. It was only when she saw his face that she let her guard down a little. That smile could still captivate her, it seems.

"James!"

"Hello there, Merry." James crossed the hall in great strides, eager to greet her. "It's still sound to call you Merry, is it?" The inquiry seemed genuine, as if he knew already that she'd had little reason to be merry these past years.

"Merry is fine." She allowed herself a little smile, which then rapidly grew into a beam, and permitted a warm hug which lingered between them, not overlong as to be unseemly, but long enough to convey the warmth of feelings that had once been between them. Withdrawing momentarily from his embrace, she glanced at that face. It seemed to Meredith that James had not aged at all. The brash confidence of that boyish smile fair swept her away as she lost herself in the better memories of Newfield.

"Merry Christmas! I was hoping you'd come, more than anyone else."

"Why, you charmer!" Meredith flushed momentarily. "I see you haven't changed much."

"Oh, you know me…" James ran his hand absently through his hair in one of his failed attempts to tame it,

"Well, I dare say I do not after all this time! We shall have to have a proper catch up! Is anyone else here? Who else was invited? I'm not quite sure how or why…"

A gravelly cough behind her gave her a second startle,

"Reckon as how I'd spoil the moment."

If James hadn't changed at all, the same could not be said for the groundskeeper, Chris. Crows' feet radiated from the corners of his small grey eyes and gave way to salt-and-pepper hair receding to a weather-beaten scalp.

"Well!" Meredith composed herself. "Another surprise. I expect this weekend will be full of them."

Chris lurched in closer, clearly slowing with age and favoring a good left leg. From his clasped hands he produced a single winter rose which he offered to Meredith with a slight nod of his head.

"I'm not much of one for hugging, but I'll offer this instead. They grow all over the back of the estate these days. It'll be a fine match for your dress."

"Thank you." Genuinely touched, but a little overwhelmed at all the sudden company after such time without it, Meredith took the flower into her own hand. "Well, then, what other surprises are in store for us?"

"Just me, I'm afraid."

All their heads turned this time and gazed up at the great stair. Descending them was another familiar face, attached to an ample frame which one might imagine belonged to a maiden aunt of the sort that kept cats or birds beyond count.

"At least as far as I'm aware."

"Ginny!" It had taken Meredith a moment - again - to recognize that face. Why did memories have to fight their way through the fog of years so? "Are you the last of our company, then?"

"I'm afraid so. No one else answered the call, it seems." She shrugged, which caused her scarf to become momentarily dislodged and caught in the balustrade. Bearing this unwarranted hiccup with good humor, Virginia reached the bottom stair. There was a brief but warm hug between them which was interrupted by James.

"Let's go through to the kitchens. It's much warmer there and Merry here is still freezing from her trip."

"The kitchens?" Meredith paused. Something wasn't quite right. "But surely..."

"No point standing on ceremony. There's only us here. We shall have to fend for ourselves! Worry not, I'm quite the dab hand." He gave her a knowing wink.

"Then the old man..." Meredith spoke barely above a whisper and allowed herself to tail off her own thought, but Ginny ran with it and replied to her.

"Gone, Dead and gone these many years, no more's the pity." Meredith detected a scowl crack across the smooth alabaster of Virginia's face.

For a moment, no one spoke. Meredith had perhaps expected one of the men to react at this breach of politeness, but it seems they were in agreement.

"Well, I shan't lose any sleep over him. Good riddance to bad blood, I say!" She took Meredith in her arm and led them both down a long oak-paneled corridor to the rear of the hall. Exchanging glances, the men followed.

"She really doesn't know?" This was from James and uttered to Chris alone as they dwindled behind the women.

"She really doesn't. That's why I called you all here, to lay this business to rest for all time."

James nodded, still uncomprehending, as they caught up and all four of them entered the kitchens.

***

When James had implied he was a dab hand, that had been an understatement. As Meredith opened the kitchen door, heady aromas began to vie for dominance in her nostrils. A heavy fragrance of cinnamon and clove from a simmering pot of mulled wine, the warm fruit of a great pudding steaming on the stove, the armfuls of fresh greens waiting to go on the hob, the delicious familiarity of a goose in the oven. Beyond those smells, a great fire burned high in the hearth such that the contrast between the chill of the great hall and the warmth of the kitchens could not be more noticeable.

Meredith sat with Virginia, who had favored them both with a glass of the mulled wine, and opposite Chris who had opened a bottle of brown ale with his knife and leaned back on the chair with his feet on the table. James busied himself with the last preparations for their Christmas feast but kept an eye and ear open on the conversations behind him.

"Oh, you must remember, Merry! It was always around Christmas that the old tyrant got so cranky. We were sure he'd be visited by ghosts himself one of those nights, just like in the story.

James had been half asleep on duty as usual"- the mock scold elicited a roaring laugh from James - "and we played a little joke. He ended up simply covered in flour - head to toe - and when the old man saw him, I thought he was going to drop dead there and then!" Ginny continued to laugh but Meredith, who had been quietly smiling along with her, suddenly stopped.

"Merry?" Virginia looked concerned. "What is it?"

"It's just that…" she sighed. "I don't remember. I can recall that we had good times here, despite the old man and his constant demands, but when I try to remember anything specific, I find that I can't. Isn't it odd?"

Chris gazed intently, continuing to drink, but said nothing. Virginia reached over and placed a reassuring hand over Meredith's, who managed a small smile at her even as a tear formed in the corner of her eye.

"Thank you. I don't know why this is so difficult. I really don't. If I can ask..." here she paused to drain her glass. "How did the old man die in the end?"

Chris slammed his empty bottle down on the table, causing both the ladies to jump out of their skins. He opened his mouth, about to say something when James interrupted cheerily.

"Dinner is served! Let's have it in here, for old time's sake."

"What do you mean?" Meredith was dizzy now, her head swirling sick not just with the cloying wine but with a heady anticipation that she was about to hear something from their past which would blow away all the fog in her mind.

"I mean, like we celebrated Christmas in the old days before the tragedy. Remember? We'd always have our meal late Christmas eve, with old master Kettle playing the fiddle while we sipped at the punch and opened our presents. It was always too busy on the day itself, with all the work involved in serving the family in their festivities."

Meredith shook with trepidation. Something formed at the back of her mind, beating on her brain as it struggled to form on her tongue.

"We were the staff? That's..."

"Whoa, quick, catch 'er!" Chris stood quickly, but not quick enough.

Virginia leapt over, just in time to catch Meredith as she slipped from her chair into a stupor.

101

"Darn it! I knew this'd be too much for her in one night." Chris swore as he strode across to open the door.

The last thing Meredith remembered that evening was James carrying her to bed, Virginia pacing just behind.

"Were? We *are* the staff. Welcome back, Meredith. Welcome home."

***

Though sleep came to Meredith swiftly, it was not restful. The fire in her room, warming at first, became all-consuming as it burned fiercer and fiercer behind the grate. Even in the dead of winter it was uncomfortably warm, and Meredith threw off her covers to cool herself down.

Then she screamed.

Under the covers with her was a single white winter rose. Not the gift Chris had given her, which still rested on her dress discarded over a footstool, but one freshly cut. As she withdrew from the bed, the covers themselves contorted into a full bloom of hellebore, encircling the whole frame and flowing free across the floor to the fire. As she stared on in disbelief, still screaming at the top of her voice, the fire roared up and swallowed the trail of flowers whole. With the bed now on fire, Meredith tried to run from the room. The door was locked. She tugged at it hopelessly, turning the knob, pulling the handle with all her might, even ringing the bell next to it. As she was about to pass out from the heat, the fire licking at the hem of her nightdress, she heard movement and shouting on the other side. Moments later, James stood there, shirtless, and breathless, the door off its hinges. But then he stood and did nothing, just looking at her quizzically.

"James, help!"

"What is it?"

"What? What do you mean, what is it?" She pushed past him into the corridor, eager to escape the inferno, as he watched in alarm.

"Merry! Merry, calm down!"

"How can I calm down when my room's on fire?"

James looked into the room. Merry looked back. There was no fire, not even in the fireplace. A single beam of moonlight shone through the drapes, perfectly illuminating the single hellebore on her dress. Merry, destroyed with grief, suddenly remembered. Waves of memories washed over her, each causing a flood of tears as she stood shivering, openly weeping now in James' embrace.

***

She stood the next morning in the garden. Chris had shown her where to find it. A single, low grave, fashioned from a crude stone and with a simple engraving. Hidden at the rear of the east wing which had once served as their quarters, she would never have managed to find it herself even if she had known it was there.

It was Virginia, not James who stood beside her here while she wept and laid a single flower upright at the base of the headstone.

ROSE HELLEBORE WINTERS
1922 TO 1938
BELOVED SISTER
"I remember now, I think. I remember it all."

As she turned to regard her, Ginny reached out her hands, which Merry grasped into hers.

"It was him, wasn't it? The old man?"

Virginia held back tears of her own. "It was. What do you remember?"

"I remember she was young. I remember he lusted for her. Wanted a little Christmas present from her. I remember I went over your head and shouted at him to leave her alone. I was furious when I found out. Unconstrained."

Virginia hung her head.

"She wasn't the first, was she?"

Virginia shook her head. The tears came unchecked now to them both. "I'm sorry. We're all sorry. We should have done more to help,"

"I understand, I think. I don't want to, but I do. Why bring me back now, though? Why have me remember?"

"It's time to move on, Merry. For all of us to move on. You know yourself that you haven't been able to, not really, until you remember."

"I think I see your point. Well, some Christmas this is turning out to be!" She was almost laughing through the tears now, hysterically. Virginia let the moment pass. "Shall we go back to the others?"

"There's one more thing."

"One more?"

Virginia looked over at her, judging the state of her well-being.

"Two." The admission came with a blush. "You asked a question last night.. Can you answer it now?"

104

"The old man. I did it, didn't I? I killed him with my own hands." She looked down at them, not in shame but in incredulity.

Virginia nodded.

"You said there were two things?"

"Look up."

Meredith raised her head high and craned her neck to look up at the east wing. Where once there had been a large building - thought nowhere near as large as the great lodge itself, there was only a ruin now. How had she not noticed this the night before when she had arrived? She struck a foot forward in tentative exploration. The charred remains of beams crushed into ash beneath her feet.

"What happened?" She knew this had to be linked to her sister somehow. She'd recalled everything else now - the good times and the bad - all those merry Christmastides they'd spent together playing and dancing and eating once the household had gone to sleep. All the arguments and staff rivalries. Her bitter condemnation of the lascivious old patriarch. But not this.

"He came looking for you both later. His rage consumed this place. We were in the servants' hall at the rear, before the great fire, roasting chestnuts."

She knew now. Knew what was coming next.

"He fell in."

"You pushed him in. We all saw. None of us stopped you."

"And then?"

"You know. Even in that state, he righted himself. You knocked him back again, but not before the fire caught hold of you too. Caught hold of the building itself. Too fast, too furious. There was no escape. No escape..."

Meredith looked down again. Behind her sister's grave, there was something else. She parted the shrubbery and knelt to rub snow from the stone.

MEREDITH "MERRY" WINTERS

1920 - 1938

DEVOTED SISTER

She looked back at Ginny for the last time. "Everyone?" she asked.

"Everyone but Chris. He slept in the gatehouse."

"Then we're..." She didn't finish. Didn't need to. It explained it all: why no one else had been invited, why there was no trace of their arrival, why none of them looked a day older.

As the two of them stood there in the early morning light, James joined them in grief and silence. They looked at each other and slowly, very slowly, began to fade from each other's view.

Behind them all, a pair of eyes surveyed them from the undergrowth, tears swelling in the corners. Chris stood watching until there was no more to see.

"God Rest Ye, Merry."

In Search of Caliph Oneiroi

Although this journal fragment is understood to document the fate of the lost 1929 expedition of Professor Flaubert, the provenance of this text cannot be verified by Miskatonic library staff. Those tests that have been carried out have confirmed that it is indeed penned with modern ink on thick papyrus. There is no entry for it in our cataloguing system, to the considerable vexation of our archivists Frey and Henley. All we can do is present the intact text below and allow the reader to draw their own conclusions.

***

We proceeded west from Cairo along a well-used trail into the desert - at night, naturally, since to begin such a journey under the glaring light of the Egyptian sun would have been sheer folly. Naturally, there were those who claimed our trip was folly anyway - a doomed expedition in search of a doomed caliph.

The night-blooming desert plants emitted a pungent, almost palpable aura which permeated the air around us. Only the chill of the night breezes kept our senses from reeling as our camel train vanished over the horizon from the city, far into the western dunes.

It was not long, I seem to recall, before our minds began playing tricks on us. We had been warned by our native guides to be alert to the mirage - that distortion and disruption of visual acuity which caused one to hallucinate through the heat haze. Pressing on through the day was not advisable in the least; indeed, we had been countenanced against such an action several times in Cairo but I was adamant that our destination would be found in one of these deserted desert valleys and that it would yield its location willingly. What utter madness! What sheer foolhardiness! I know that now - and much more besides - and wish that I would have known it then.

When the day was nearly spent, we spied a light shimmering in the distance and instantly dismissed it as one of those selfsame mirages which had plagued us under the harsh sun. Directionless and with our sight dimming in the darkness, we decided to head for it anyway; the only point of light save the stars on a sand-strewn ocean of utter darkness.

As we approached the apparition only grew in strength; its very existence was indeed firmly rooted in our reality. A lone bell tolled from the gatepost; echoing eerily even given the distance yet to cross and beckoning, beckoning, with its discordant yet somehow somnolent tones. Our heads grew heavy as we drew near and it was then we first spied the strange figure waiting for us in the doorway of what appeared to be the palace of a local potentate, somehow incongruously situated here in the deep desert. Was this indeed much wanted respite for a needy traveler? Or some fresh hell perpetrated on our senses? I considered these options as I surveyed the wonders of the courtyard. It was indeed a lovely place, lonely but welcoming in its way as was the countenance of the young lady who greeted us. With a coy smile, she lit a single candle which burned brightly in the umbral gloom and beckoned us in, indicating that there was plenty of space inside for us to rest.

The corridor from the courtyard to the interior was lined with ancient statues fashioned to resemble the gods of the pantheon of ancient Egypt which had first captured my imagination as a small boy. I looked at each of their shadowed forms in wonder as we proceeded to what I took as a lobby. As I did so, I reeled in shock as the whispered winds through their stately forms carried words which, in hindsight, we should have known to be warning.

"Welcome," they seemed to say. I knew it to be problematic in the highest order for those words to be uttered in the mother tongue of old London, but I remained fascinated, unwilling, and obstinate, not willing to give up what might be a vital - as well as excellent - place to take in water and sustenance for any further ventures into the inhospitable landscape which surrounded us.

"You will always find welcome here." I could no longer tell if the voice was emanating from those ancient Pharaonic forms which adorned the lobby or whether they issued forth from the lips of our erstwhile hostess. As she ushered us, exhausted and limp from our travails, through the lobby to an inner courtyard, I was struck by the impossibility that not only were there other guests but that each of them was a veritable symbol of virility; Nubian warriors conjured forth from the depths of time each of their semi-naked forms rippling with musculature from headdress to golden loincloth. Each of them was seemingly lost in a trance, undulating away to piped music bidden from the recesses of their own minds, glistening with sweat even in the depths of night.

Parched as I was, I inquired what refreshment might be had; all other considerations of this mysterious and forbidding place could wait until my addled pate had been restored by refreshing liquid sustenance which we had rigorously rationed during our trip. It was evident from her reply that such blessed waters were not currently available, and I had to avail myself of the remainder of my own waterskin just to keep my thinking clear as I was shown to the most sumptuous bedroom I have encountered outside of the hotels of Bohemia. Even as I slept, the voices continued to plague me. Had I heeded their warning earlier, I might have come fully to my senses and torched the place for the den of madness and iniquity it was, but alas this was not the case.

I awoke, somewhat refreshed after a disturbing night's sleep, but famished. Since no staff saw fit to disturb my quarters, I dressed and began to pace the rich, carpeted halls of the palace, idly wandering through room after room, all jeweled and filigree beyond the ransom of a king, but empty, so empty. Mirrors adorned the ceilings, distorted reflections of my haggard form staring back at me with wasting, wanting eyes, locked in a horror of their own remembrance of better days. It then occurred to me to check on the camels, but I was unable to find the exit to the lobby. Each room distorted dimensions to such an extent that I, and those other admirable companions who had accompanied the expedition and since joined me in my increasingly desperate meanderings through this golden nightmare, were utterly, dejectedly lost.

Our exploration continued at a frenzied pace, keen to avoid the gazes of our mirrored forms bearing down upon us and fearing for our sanity, knowing that we were now likely prisoners here of our own folly and guilelessness. We finally came - by design it seemed - to a chamber that was different from the others, in which sat all of those nubile Nubian men we had seen the night before, swaying gently in cacophonous prayers which tugged the cords of our now-frail mental faculties. At the center of this circle sat a bearded figure richly dressed in satins and silks with a large tome resting on his ample lap. Here he was! The object of our search, the dread Caliph Oneiroi, the Sender of Dreams. We were utterly unprepared, having been drawn to this very room at the heart of his strength, at his very bidding. As we entered, he looked up at us with grey, forbidding eyes and uttered a single word, a final pronouncement of doom upon the remainder of our lives. The pages of the book fluttered and from them arose a squamous, misshapen form which defied all description. As it oozed and slithered toward us, we readied what weapons we had; knives of steel with which we tried to penetrate its thick, rubbery hide to no avail. Whatever this loathsome abomination was, we could not even injure it and were forced to retreat in haste as waves of blistering insanity finally overtook us.

The last thing I recall was a hasty rush to the door - a last, desperate hope of escape. I must find the passage back to our own reality! To the normalcy of the desert heat, the call of the muezzins in that now far-off city where we had started this foolish escapade! As we ran pell-mell from the umbral tentacles, through room after identical room, we knew we were doomed. A numbness overcame us, a desire to remain here in perpetuity, to relax and give in to the worst excesses of our minds and become as one with the horror of the uncaring, inhospitable universe and its dark, terrible secrets. It seemed we could never leave now, but with one last great surge of will, we finally managed to triumph. When we turned around, the palace was no more.

Lord of the Dance

I Danced In The Morning

They gather in their masses as he looks on from a nearby rooftop, restringing his violin and letting his bare feet dangle precariously over the edge to the packed streets below. Soon he will take his place at the head of the crowd and strike a tune, leading them on a merry procession through the city streets. For now, he appears content to watch the throng assemble in the main square, a panoply of masked and costumed partygoers, ready for a day of fun.

As he stares down at them, one of them looks back and points up excitedly, nudging two of her friends and waving up at him from far below. He allows himself a polite wave and a bow, his fiddle flashing in the bright light of the morning sun. Then he withdraws from the edge to a small sack which contains his patchwork partywear and begins to climb into the voluminous robe.

On with the motley.

***

"I swear to you, that's him, look!" Sandra shielded her eyes against the sun and squinted back up at the figure on the rooftop. Removing his mask, a serious young man next to her tried to match her line of sight.

"I can't see anything. Are you sure?"

"He's gone now, but he was there, I swear! That must be a good omen, to see him early! He even

113

bowed at me!" Her companion side-eyed her skeptically then nudged the third of their group.

"Looks like the heat's got to Sandra already! Seeing things in the heat haze." He wiped matted black hair from his brow. "I'm going to keep my mask off until we start. It's way too hot to be wearing it already."

"That's bad luck." Sandra frowned, then looked dejectedly back at the roof.

"Y'know, I did see something. Maybe it was him. I've only seen a picture of him in the brochure though and whoever that was up there was wearing something quite different. But still..." Toby, the third of their party, craned his head again. Sandra smiled at him, glad to have a co-conspirator, even a half-hearted one. He snapped his neck back. "Anyone fancy a beer? There's a little bar on the plaza a couple of roads over, we could chill there in the shade rather than sweat ourselves to death here."

"I told Libby we'd meet her here." Marcus looked around and shrugged. "Not that she'd be able to spot us in this madness at any rate."

Sandra didn't dwell on why Libby and Marcus hadn't arrived together but did exchange a meaningful glance with Toby. *I hope everything's OK between them.* Toby shrugged in response. *I just wish he'd lighten up; it's supposed to be a party for goodness' sake.* "I'll text her. Come on. Let's see if there are still places to sit down, there'll be plenty of time to stand up later."

***

Dance, then, wherever you may be

114

His fingers were ever straying and impatient to be playing.

What lives have these people led? How empty must those lives be that they flock to this one particular place on this one particular day just to 'have fun'? Can merriment not be sought in other places, at other times? If people felt it necessary to have a season to be jolly, what did that say about their temperaments the rest of the time?

He knew this to be the case even as he rosined up his bow. He knew the indignities mankind inflicted on one another, hour after hour, day after day. It wasn't a surprise when you had been watching them, in one guise or another, for millennia.

Today he would lead them all away from this. Let them lose themselves in little moments of joy and ecstasy. Take them back to those rare and precious times, often in their childhood, when ignorance was bliss.

It wasn't that they deserved it, far from it. It was just what he did.

He opened up his case and said, "I'll start this show."

***

Sandra took one look at Libby as she approached and sighed audibly. Libby wound her way across the crowded plaza where the others sat at one of the trestle tables set up earlier that morning, under the shade of a giant yellow umbrella proudly emblazoned with the name of a beer none of them had ever heard of and were unlikely to drink if there weren't free samples given out to all the festival goers.

115

Libby tripped over four or five times on her way to them, each time cursing the ground she walked on, her shoes, nearby patrons, whatever seemed appropriate. Sandra wondered whether she was incredibly hung over or still drunk and guessed this had been the source of the sourness she had detected with Marcus earlier. Whichever it was, it was going to cast a shadow over their whole day.

Libby waved hello as she spotted them and drew nearer. Her eyes were hidden behind mirrored sunglasses and the rest of her face was hidden in the shade of a wide brimmed bright yellow sun hat from the rear of which protruded a few stray blonde strands. She blew a kiss at a nearby waiter as she grabbed one of the promotional beers from the tray and sat down next to Marcus. As Libby lit a cigarette and began to speak, Sandra could smell the tequila lingering on her breath from the night before.

"You left us early last night, Marcus! You missed the best bit of the party!"

Marcus squirmed his hand away as Libby attempted to grab it. Having failed, her limp wrist was left dangling over the side of the table, a golden bracelet flashing in the midday sun.

"Ooh, what happened?" Sandra was in no mood for this bullshit. Calling Libby out now was the best way to shut her up and a sullen, pouty Libby would be a better companion than the full-tilt party girl persona Libby liked to put on for an audience.

"Well, er, lots of stuff." Sandra smiled inside; as she thought, Libby had been too out of it to know. Probably still was. "Some of the musicians from the

116

carnival joined us late, must have been about three in the morning. They played all night. All night, Marcus!" One last attempt at attention. It failed. Marcus had already withdrawn into the text of the festival brochure.

Libby downed her beer in one and then signaled for another. Sandra, after a moment's thought, did the same. If you can't beat them, join them.

***

I'll lead you all in the Dance

The procession snaked endlessly down Main Street, ebbing and flowing with the mass of sweaty flesh. He crooked his neck, just once, to check they were following him and flash them a knowing smile from beneath his quartered red and yellow mask. He pulled the strings across the bow and it gave an evil hiss. As it did, barely discernible wisps of yellow smoke began to issue from it and waft their way behind him into the madding crowd.

It hadn't always been the violin he'd used as an instrument of temptation, far from it. Hundreds of years ago, the flute was the instrument of jollity he'd used to draw a crowd. He still carried that at his side; not in case the fiddle failed to enthrall - it never had - but as a reminder of the power he had once wielded, and the lessons humanity had yet to learn:

Always pay the piper.

Always give the devil his due.

Otherwise, all hell will break loose.

***

"I am *not* drunk!" Libby lashed out as Marcus tried to catch her, but promptly lost her balance and

117

fell over sideways into a trash can. Sandra, surprising herself, erupted in fits of laughter. Marcus' face was a contorted mask of rage and frustration which had already progressed from *'you're embarrassing me'* to *'I'm not talking to you anymore.'* Toby just gazed stoically, arms folded, more annoyed that they were losing sight of the front of the parade where the musician was.

Since none of them seemed willing to help her up, Libby struggled to gain her own footing, which she managed on the third attempt. Sandra has finished laughing by then but remained strangely mesmerized by her own choice of action not moments before. Composing herself, she held out a tanned forearm for Libby to grasp as she righted herself. Libby glowered crossly at her, refusing it, but changed her mind as she continued to wobble. She now reeked of tequila and garbage. Though in Sandra's mind, Libby had always been garbage.

"Shall we?" Toby unfolded his arms and found a way for them through the closeness of the crowd, determined to have his fun that day regardless of what the others did.

"Wait up!" Marcus ran to him, out of breath even after a few paces. Sandra didn't hear what they said to each other as she was busy helping Libby divest herself of a few items of trash that had somehow made their way onto her ensemble. Though, still feeling puckish, she decided to leave the banana peel on her sun hat. Toby and Marcus shared a brief laugh and then high-fived each other. Toby pulled something out of his shirt pocket which glinted briefly - *tin foil maybe? She wasn't really paying attention* - and they both took a pinch of something from it. Sandra sighed, reaching for her hip flask. Damned if she was going to be the only adult in the room yet again.

***

I am the Dance and I still go on

He turned a corner and led the merrymakers away from the main drag down toward the docks via a circuitous route through high-sided office blocks which then gave way to the warehouse district. There were less people watching from the doors and windows here but that wasn't important. Everyone he wanted had already joined the dance. They moved behind him as a mass of masked faces, each hiding their own thoughts, their own dreams. He chose not to care what those were. Not this time. He wanted them to think as one, move as one, act as one. A single huddled orchestra for him to conduct. What to him if their cacophony was unmelodic, their speaking and shrieking and squeaking in fifty different sharps and flats? He was the Dance itself, the dance of life and death, and his tune carried throughout the eons, a drum beat that pounded through history.

Around him, two circles of dancers began to writhe to his never-ending tune, finding their own rhythms in the procession. As others surged forward, they formed one of these ever-expanding spirals, which fanned out onto the promenade, the boardwalk, the docks and even some of the little jetties that jutted out into the quietly lapping water.

One circle moved slowly, clockwise, swaying slightly, their hands dipping and then rising in

119

unison, prostrating themselves before him before picking themselves up. They fanned themselves out and began a gentle to-and-fro toward the rest of the approaching crowd. Their masks, everyone, were sickly shades of yellow.

The other circle started as slow but rapidly picked up speed. Theirs was not the languid rhythm of the yellow masks - their masks were deep hues of crimson and scarlet and they swayed frenetically from side to side, whirling like dervishes as they spun outwards.

Perfectly still, in the center of the storm, the lord of the dance played on.

***

Libby hung over the iron railings which sealed the street from an alley full of broken bottles and broken dreams, retching repeatedly until her stomach was empty. Sandra looked on, no longer laughing but not caring either. Her own eyes were glazed over, and she looked longingly down at her empty hip flask. She began to feel ill both from the vodka she had drained and the awful reek of Libby's vomit which had completely ruined both their dresses. The guys were nowhere to be seen, not that either of them had noticed. She was about to say something to Libby when she heard screams begin to erupt from the crowd nearer the docks. Not the whooping and the hollering that had accompanied the procession, but full-throated shrieks of horror. She left the barely conscious Libby behind and climbed a nearby fire escape to get a better view.

"We've lost the girls."

"Huh?" Marcus looked up from the brochure again and over at Toby. He squinted slightly - Toby seemed to be enveloped in a subtle swirl of sickly colors as flesh- and blood-hued wisps began to encircle him.

"I said, we've lost the girls." Toby looked worried. How long ago had they lost sight of them? Was it round the last corner? The crowd was pushing forward so quickly now and carrying them with it as the masses dispersed onto the waterfront. Toby wrenched the brochure from Marcus's hand and forced him to pay attention. "What is it with you and this brochure?"

"I've been trying to figure it out...the route we've taken is different to the one listed. Look..." He grabbed the brochure back and opened it up full size to reveal the whole map. "We've gone down this way - Bedeil Street - rather than down Sarbarret." Marcus traced the new route on the map with his finger. He was alarmed to notice that he had pricked it somehow; there was a thin trickle of blood on the map. Then the map shuddered violently, distorting, and contorting in his fingertips. Toby looked on in shock.

"Are... er... are you seeing what I'm seeing? It's...oh wow it's beautiful."

Marcus wasn't seeing it at all anymore. The blood had welled up behind his eyes and now flowed freely as he cried bright red tears. Clutching his face, he dropped the map and fell to the floor.

"Whoa."

***

I am the life that'll never never die

121

His queer long coat from heel to head was half of yellow and half of red. He himself was tall and thin with sharp blue eyes each like a pin.

He smiled. He hadn't felt so alive since Hamelin.

That was him. The life of the party. Its pulse. Its heart blood. The Dance giveth and the Dance taketh away. Blessed be the Dance which creates and destroys both, which bringeth all things into being and finally undoes the illusion, releasing the souls of mankind from their purgatories of flesh.

And now for the finale.

***

"Marcus. Babes. Pick up." Libby could barely breathe let alone speak, but she'd managed one speed dial as she tried to climb over the railings to get away from the press of the crowd.

"Help, dammit!" She shook the phone in her hand as she was pushed back to the side of the street again when the throng surged past her once more.

"Hey! Watch what you're doing!"

"Libby!" She spun round, trying to find who had called her name. Her heart was beating fast now, her head spinning.

"Up here!"

Libby craned her neck, shielding her eyes against the sun. She had lost the shades and the hat somewhere around the third bout of vomiting. She could barely make out Sandra's shape three floors up, leaning against a fire escape and pointing excitedly up toward the waterfront.

"Get up here! I can see everything! Everything!" This last word was spoken slowly, tapering off into

122

a distorted jangle of syllables Libby strained to understand.

"I know, Libby! I know!" Sandra's face, not that Libby could see it that clearly, was locked in beatific rapture. She tottered slightly as she tried to reach down to Libby three stories below.

"Sandy! Watch out!" Libby tried - far too late - to sober up, Sandra couldn't see everything, she reckoned. She couldn't see the strange vermillion clouds gathering overhead or the way the office blocks were slowly transforming into jagged sheets of humming crystal. Nevertheless, she tried to reach up - three stories wasn't that far, was it? It felt a lot closer than that - and then they would be able to connect again. The last she saw of Sandra was the look on her face when the ground shook beneath them, rocking the fire escape and sending her hurtling down, down, down with a look not of panic but serene beauty.

She took a long time to fall - much longer than Libby thought given that they were so close only a moment ago - their fingertips were nearly touching! Libby didn't have much time to react though as the roaring crowd forced her body against a new growth of crystal shards which impaled her clean through. Her corpse twitched twice as the spiky crystal continued to grow through her. The crowd went wild.

Marcus pounded his fists hard against Toby's soft, yielding, flesh as he knelt over him on the street, letting the crowd trample over and past them. Toby was covered in his own blood now but still lay prone on the floor. The procession ignored them both, not that there was much of a carnival left - Marcus could just make out from his red-dimmed eyes that a number of similar fights seemed to have broken out. He turned his attention back to his prey and began to sink his teeth into Toby's shoulder as his hands reached down into Toby's shirt pocket where the little packets of yellow powder were still wrapped in their individual tin foil wraps. Marcus swallowed them all in one gulp, roared in triumph as he threw Toby's lifeless form to the baying mob and then pounced on another nearby partygoer, knocking him to the street and caving his skull in on the cobblestones. As the frenzied throng finished devouring his friend's body, the red clouds parted to a sickly yellow sky over a rugged landscape of crystalline formations towering forever upward.

The city and its people were no more.

***

I am the Lord of the Dance

What next? Where next?

There is no what or where really, not to the Lord of the Dance. Nor a when. There is only one choice: What tune shall they dance to next?

Memento Mori

He likes to make us dance. Every night, he sits cross-legged on a tomb and pulls out a little flute of carved bone wrapped in... let's call it leather. He puts it to his cracked lips and begins to play. Across the cemetery, hands force their way through disturbed dark earth, yearning to be free, their nails stained by the escape from their eternal prisons. What ragged, filthy flesh remains stretches upward, dragging flaccid corpses into the chill night. Those of us who have been dead longer rise slower, bone-bleached, and cantankerous, and rattle our way up to join this processional of the damned, bound in service to an ancient eldritch tool now in the unworthiest of hands.

He forces me to lead, on account of my former occupation at the court, he says. I stumble and shake as the grisly parade begins, shuffling around the graveyard with no purpose other than to titillate the despotic mind of an assured lunatic. The houses he makes do not last till doomsday: they are temporary resting places only. We rarely have the fortune to end the parade in the same patch of earth in which we start.

When I first tried to rebel, to rail against this shambolic reminder of life, he removed my skull as punishment. He likes to show it to people occasionally. Not that visitors to the graveyard are frequent. "Quite as the grave". Ha! There is nothing quiet about this mockery of life: a clacking of old bones, the soft plop of sloughing, rancid flesh as it hits the soft earth, and above all the manic laughter of the gravedigger himself.

The dead hunger not for blood or revenge, but for rest. We are all prisoners of that unquiet mind, void of meaning. I had a tongue in me and could sing once. I was thought of as a fellow of infinite jest. Now there are no flashes of merriment left.

Alas.

Midnight Rider

"Listen my children and you shall hear!" The crowd hushed and shuffled closer as he began. "They say he rides out at midnight. The same night every year. The same night as his first fateful ride. Tonight."

Brett's voice was hushed, partially to keep up the mystique of his own storytelling and partially because he was carried away in the narrative himself. There was a small crowd gathered round him, hanging on his every word. At least, that's what he assumed. There was very little to see in the gloom of an overcast east coast evening, especially this far out of town. But he had takings for forty people in his back pocket (cash only, it was always cash only) so he figured he had forty people. In the distance to the north were a few flickering headlights and occasional traffic noises from the highway. To the east, the Boston skyline was illuminated by the suffused glow of light rain and the moonlight flowing overall. He hoped the signal system would still work as Amy said it would. They hadn't really had a chance to test it properly when they'd come up with this ghost walk shtick.

Too late to worry now. Brett was pretty confident he could wing it. It was his story, after all, and his carefree sing-song voice doing the telling. He warmed to the feel of the rapt crowd even as he huddled further in his greatcoat, the damp of the river fog clinging to his lanky frame. The crowd were the only thing warming him at the moment; later it would be good beer, good company and then just him and Amy.

"Shhhh." The crowd had picked up a little low chatter while Brett had been lost in his own thoughts. "Now look to the east. You can just make the city out through the rain - that's it over there. We have another member of the team on active standby. She'll warn us when the horseman is about to start out towards us. Look up, you'll see what I mean."

Brett fumbled in his coat pocket for his phone. Without removing it from his pocket, he pressed a single button to send a message, all the time with his eyes firmly on the shape of the crowd all craning their necks without knowing exactly why.

Putty in my hands.

***

Amy's phone buzzed angrily on the rail beside her, almost knocking itself to the floor and definitely waking her up. She rubbed her eyes to reacquaint herself with the near darkness of the bell tower and suddenly remembered what she was there for as she saw the single word of Brett's text message.

NOW

Damn it, Brett, you're early. Couldn't you have kept them talking for just a little longer? She reached down through a tangle of cables to where two powerful lamps were perched on the windowsill and hit the ON switches. After that, she reckoned

128

she'd have about a minute before the lamps began to attract the attention of the authorities. If everything went to plan, by then they would have done their job and she could turn them off in time. If not… well she preferred not to think about that, but she did have a nearby bolt hole just in case. She was a lot more prepared than Brett. She had to be really, because as cute as he was Brett was a dreamer, not a thinker.

She reached down and flicked the switch. There was a low hum as the lights began to power up, but apart from that there was only the secret dread of the lonely belfry.

***

The crowd let loose with a loud "Oooh!". Brett looked up with them and was surprised at the light he saw coming from the church.

Nice work, Amy! Wow, that really is atmospheric. He'd been worried that the lamps she'd borrowed from their roadie friend wouldn't be up to the task, but clearly, she'd surpassed herself. Not only were they bright enough to breach the long distance from the city, she'd also managed to rig them with some muted blue-green filter which permeated through the rain and even penetrated the mist down here by the river, lending an extra layer of spookiness to the scene.

"The beacons are lit!" His cry cut through the murmurs of his audience and a ripple of silence passed over them. He lowered his own voice to meet it. "Follow me if you please. That's right, slowly now, we don't want anyone slipping in the mud. Quietly, thank you, yes, let's keep the noise

129

down as much as we can. We don't want to scare the ghost, after all." As they trudged forward, Brett fumbled once more for his cellphone and sent a second text to a different number. Irritatingly, he saw he'd missed a call from Amy, who was supposed to be maintaining radio silence. He briefly wondered if she was in any trouble but decided to press on regardless. He'd find a way to call her quickly when the crowd were distracted by the sight of the midnight rider.

**

Jason swore under his breath as his phone buzzed. He'd been sitting here for nearly an hour now and in his boredom had taken to smoking a joint. Beside him, the horse he'd 'borrowed' from the Van Tassel stables whinnied softly. Whatever it was saying, it seemed to be about as impressed by the weather as he was. Stamping out his smoke on the damp ground, he checked the incoming message.

YOU'RE UP

Well, then. Time to freak out some unsuspecting rubes. He managed to mount the horse easily enough and set them into an easy but slow trot. The bioluminescent paint - also 'borrowed' - still covered parts of them both even though the perpetual light rain had washed some of it off. He hoped that what remained was enough, then remembered that Brett was paying him the same cut regardless and relaxed further, intent on enjoying himself whatever the weather.

130

As they clopped forward, however, Jason saw something which set them on a different path altogether.

***

The crowd shuffled forward, keeping to a low hush. Brett had allowed them to push forward without him, the lantern he'd hung at the edge of the little bridge clearly visible now and marking the point where they'd be able to spot Jason on the opposite bank. When they were all in front, he took out his cellphone again and, his face lit eerily by the screen, listened to whatever it was Amy had been so keen to tell him.

"Brett? Brett! Oh my god, Brett please pick up! That wasn't me! I don't know what the fu… Shit, there's someone coming. Brett, you there? Help! The lamps didn't work. I don't know what happened, but all of a sudden there were these other lights and…oh god, someone's knocking on the door, what should I do? Brett, pick up, please? Please! I'm so scared. There must be two or three of them right outside the door, I've got nowhere to go, my dad'll kill me, there's…"

There then followed an almighty crashing sound which Brett figured must be the door being broken down. The last thing he heard Amy call out before she was cut off was something about them coming for her. After that everything went dead.

It was at that point, down by the bridge, that the screaming began.

***

"Whoa! WHOA!"

131

The first of these exclamations was an instruction from Jason to his ignoble steed. The second was more of a panicked utterance as he tried desperately to get away. The air around him suddenly crackled with fearful energies which caused his horse to rear uncontrollably and snort in sheer terror. Then, seemingly from out of nowhere, the mist nearby coalesced into the spectral form of a man on a horse, which also reared as if in response to his own. Unlike Jason's horse, though, this spectral stallion appeared triumphant rather than terrified. As the man's head turned toward them, Jason saw straight through it to the woods beyond and decided that's where he'd rather be. Trying desperately to bring his own mount under control, Jason failed and then flailed as it threw him ignominiously to the ground as it raced off as fast as its legs could carry it. The last thing Jason remembered seeing before he passed out was a swift procession of twig, shrub and root as his head hit the ground with a thud. The last thing he heard was an echoing neigh as the rider urged his mount onwards to an unseen rendezvous, tricorn raised in his left hand as he held the reins in his right, and then the tramp of his steed as he rode forth. Behind and beyond that were the faint blares of trumpets, then only the pumping of his own heart and his frantic breaths, then nothing.

***

Brett panicked as he raced toward the ghost tour group. If he'd have known what was happening, if he'd have thought for a moment, he might have headed the other way. He might even have heeded his own advice about moving slowly so as not to fall over in the murk and the dark. Fat chance of that now. Half the crowd came hurtling toward him through the brush; the rest had scattered in other directions. Boots trampled, feet entangled, bodies fell to the ground. Brett himself was knocked over in the rush and by the time he had picked himself back up he was the only one remaining.

Except for the unexpected guest.

Unexpected was the right word. He'd never really believed the stories himself, beyond skimming the basis of the legend enough to run this scam. All he really knew was that the figure on the ghostly horse now gazing down at him was a most revered historical figure. He began to scramble backwards on his mud-stricken hands as full panic settled in. He was close enough to make out the horse's breath, distinct from the mist by its vague pale blue glow. He was close enough to see the whites of the rider's eyes as they narrowed on him and to hear his voice raised in anger.

"What manner of man are you, sir?"

Brett tried to raise a word in response, but nothing came out. He had given up trying to stand now but was still frantically trying to crawl backwards on only his hands and rear. He was not getting very far.

"I said, sir, who are you? To whom do you owe your loyalty?"

Brett faltered. "I...I, oh god please don't hurt me, let me go please. I'll give the money back. I didn't mean it! Just a harmless prank!" Brett was quick-witted enough to know that this wasn't what he needed or meant to say, but in fear his words betrayed his heart.

The rider paused for a moment. Brett looked around him. The fog in the whole of the little hollow the brook ran through had taken on a faint blue tinge now, like the horse's breath. He suddenly realized that the darkness was at once more and less intense than it had previously been, and it took him a moment to understand why.

The two bright lanterns, - lit by someone other than Amy, apparently - were no longer there. Neither were any of the distant suffused lights of the city. That accounted for the darkness. Above him, though, the sky shone with the brilliance of more stars than he'd ever seen at once, accompanied by a full, gleaming moon.

What the fuck?

The rider looked down at him again, this time in pity more than fury. "I have no time for you, stranger. I must away, my task this night cannot be delayed. Pray they do not find you, whoever you may be."

Brett managed to blurt out one question quickly as the rider turned his horse around.

"Who do you mean by 'they?'"

The rider regarded him incredulously.

"The regulars, man! The regulars are coming!" This he spoke as his gallop began anew, fearless and fleet, even as Brett could hear the approach of hooves in pursuit behind him and spy a flash of red coats among the trees before he was overwhelmed by the experience and he lost consciousness, alone in the dark and the rain and fog.

***

"There's your share."

Amy, huddled into a deep blue hoodie, stretched forth a single freckled arm, pale and shaking. Framing her face through the depths of the cowl were locks of white hair. They had not been there before, and Brett dared not ask just what she'd seen. Heaven knows he'd seen enough.

"It's not about the money, Brett." But she took it anyway. She hadn't asked Brett what had happened either. She'd barely made it back to the coffee shop herself in time after the church bells had woken her at midday. He didn't seem much affected, but she knew that not to be the case. She always knew with Brett. He'd taken a few knocks in his life, but he'd always managed to get back on his feet. She wasn't sure this time.

"Sure. I mean, it never is, right? Not really. It's about the thrill of the chase." He took the opportunity to smile, but it came out fake somehow. He averted his gaze from hers and stared out the window into the damp air of a Boston afternoon.

"Nobody contacted me. No reviews, nothing. You'd think, since I'd given them the real deal, they'd be a…"

"Cut it, Brett, I don't have time for this today. Whatever happened had best stay quiet, between us. Not that there's those who'd believe us. Not really."

Brett's eyes flashed alive for the first time since they'd met today. "Oh, sure they will. There will be plenty more. It's all in the telling of the story, you see?" He stood, wobbling slightly, and coughed

135

loudly for attention. The coffee shop patrons turned toward him.

"Listen my children and you shall hear!"

Amy sighed and took another sip of her coffee.

Sang-froid

They don't tell you about the cold. They don't need to. Everyone knows it's cold. Anyway, it's not the measurements of the thermometer that are important. Not to people, anyway. It's what the cold *does* to you that matters.

Franklin stands patiently on the deck, looking out across a sea of white. No speck of foliage to break the monotony. No promontory of grey stone to act as a landmark, just an endless sea of pack ice.

They don't tell you about the silence either. No birdsong, No insects. The reason they don't tell you is that it isn't silent. The pack ice itself fills in the gaps that the rest of nature has left absent. It howls, it sizzles, it cracks, it yowls and screams; it is thunder, it is driving rain, it is the beating sun for a land and a sea that knows none of these things.

It is because of this ice that their ship, the Erebus, is trapped; their very mission under threat. A deadly labyrinth of shifting floes, cracking and reforming. He knows now that the glory will not be his. He knows the price he must pay for his folly.

Franklin is haunted. By his own ambition, by the imperial hubris of the former captain and his botanist. But most of all by the tiny spider-like creatures they discovered in the hold. Creatures the Erebus must have picked up on its former voyage - a voyage to Antarctica, about as far away from their current location as is humanly possible.

137

These guests, so tiny as to be near-invisible, even before you take into account that they are translucent as if fashioned from the very ice itself, are possessed of a singular collective mind. An intelligence to match the brain of any respected scientist. A persistent constitution enough to match that of the most stalwart explorer. They have devastated the hold supplies. They have spewed forth across his body, burying themselves within his clothing and within the very folds of his flesh, deeper, deeper, deeper until they find blood.

His blood coagulates on the slightest wound, like the shaving cut he accidentally delivered yesterday. It freezes on contact with the air, flecks of ice glistening on his skin while the tiny spiders run over and under his skin, working their way through his flesh and his resolve in equal measure.

For days now, the howls of these minute monstrosities have dug themselves into his mind, permeating the very core of his being. Yet he persists. He stands stoically, sucking on his pipe, staring across the never-ending bleakness of his world, which fascinates and horrifies in equal measure.

Franklin knows the time has come. He will not be marked by his failure, but by his strength. His cold, rational decisions. When he acts, he knows that it will save his crew - for now, at least. He reaches into his greatcoat and digs out his journal, glancing over it as if it were an object foreign to him now. He must record his decision. His crew must never know what he is about to do - or why - lest they mark themselves unwillingly as prey for the crawling chaos that plays out under his skin. But others must know. Will know. When it is found, there will be lectures given in the (natural societies) about its contents and their meaning. Those things man was not meant to know will be known. There is so much they still do not understand, and will not until science has advanced to the point where these things can be studied, calculated, prevented...

And until humanity has understood that they are not alone. That these tiny minds are, in concert, equal to ours, and just as unthinking, conquering, blindly malevolent in their actions.

It is a matter of honour. It is a matter of sacrifice.

Franklin edges forward. One moment - a singular fraction of hesitation in a mind ridden with desperation and resolve alike.

"And now, we commit this body to the deep..."

Splash.

She Sells Seashells

I often saw her plying her wares. She would walk along the seafront, as bright and breezy as the weather and the weekend crowds drawn down from the capital by the new railway.

Until, one day, I didn't.

There were rumors she had succumbed to an illness, though as the town's foremost physician I found this remarkably hard to believe. The partaking of regular sea air and seawater had been a well-recognized tonic here since the days of Dr. Russell's patent medicines.

Her wheelbarrow still stood on the promenade, though it was starkly empty of wares. I wondered what might have caused her to abandon it. While I feared for her safety, others feared for my sanity, I had stopped promenading and started patrolling. I stopped passersby and, armed only with a frayed photograph, began asking questions.

"Excuse me, have you seen this girl?"

The answer was most often a firm shake of the head accompanied by an associated melancholy which seemed to ask me a question back:

"Why this one? With the tide of humanity ebbing and flowing from the capital to the beaches and back, what was particular about this one person?"

Sometimes that was asked of me and sometimes I asked it of myself. I continued my practice, dispensing proprietary medicines of the sort Russell would have been proud of. Occasionally, when I ventured to the shore for more seawater, I lingered overlong and stared out, standing at that sacred time between the day and the night at that sacred place between the land and the sea. I had made a good living from it; I didn't deny that. I took those precious life-giving waters and used them to make a real change in the world. Yet there was always something fearful about those waters even when they were placid. When they were full of fury, they might devour the whole town without a second thought.

I looked back to those fishing boats still moored at the hard scrabble above the high tide mark and something struck me.

They would know.

I'd spent so much time asking tourists that I'd neglected those that knew too well how fickle a mistress the sea might be and here they were, huddled around a little fire on the beach to keep warm. Time has not been kind to our ever-dwindling fleet, the wind and water had not been kind to their pock-marked and weather-beaten faces. Still, I was familiar to them after a fashion and was in sore need of company who might understand.

There was a shift in their temperament as I approached them. I thought for a moment there might be violence. My mind shuddered at the fate of our seashell seller and whether they had a part in it. Was I about to talk to friend or foe? There seemed no way to find out but to ask.

The fisherfolk were fortified with concoctions stronger than I had ever prepared and many of them were reeling drunk. Still, they listened to my impassioned entreaties and let me finish before they replied.

"Aye, we know her." One stood, a man rougher and older than his companions. Grey flecked his beard; rum flecked his lips. He seemed unsteady on his feet, though I daresay I would be equally unsteady bobbing up and down in his little fishing boat. "Tho' we ain't seen her in these parts for near a month. Strange little thing... She kept 'erself to 'erself, took no boat but ne'er came back on an evening with aught less than a full haul. Many's a time we wondered where her spot was, but she never did tell. No, sir, she never did tell. Reckon as she'll come back?"

I replied in the negative and between us we allowed ourselves a moment which we both spent avoiding the impropriety of shedding a tear. Thanking them for their time and their honesty, I withdrew and made my way back along the beach, lost in thought as the stones crunched beneath my feet and the waves lapped softly in the distance.

At that juncture, I heard her voice calling. I swear till this day it was her voice I heard, so help me God, and I'll never forget the words she spoke.

"I can't take any more."

I whirled round, stumbling a little - I thoroughly admit this was out of fright and in no part due to the modicum of rum of which I had recently partaken - and tried to find a place for that melody of melancholy.

Nothing.

My senses reeling now from more than liquor, I tried to still the rapid beating of my heart.

"I can't take any more."

Again, that plaintive cry. Again, I tried to find the source and could only conclude it came from the ocean itself. I stepped forward with more bravado than I would have credited myself. I must know the answer to this mystery. Heavens, she might be injured! Was this the cry of a maiden in distress? Or the last gasp of a desperate suicide?

Before I knew it, I stood at the very edge of the water, waves breaking around my feet, and called out her name.

Silence.

I tried again. What I heard call back frightens me still to this day.

"And neither can you."

A great wave washed over me, drenching me in more brine than I sold in a week. I ran.

That voice was not hers. I would never hear her voice again, I know that now, unless I succumbed to the same call which had taken her.

The ocean knows.

It knows who has taken from it and it exacts a price for that taking. A reckoning of sorts. It giveth forth, but it also taketh away.

The following morning, I hung a 'closed' sign over the door of my business and took the railway to the capital. Never again would I set foot on the shore.

The Watcher in the Well

For as long as I had been visiting my grandmother's rural retreat, there remained a singular object of fascination to me. It was an old stone well, situated in the grounds at the rear of the property, overgrown with weeds. When I was younger, scrabbling through the undergrowth to find it was the highlight of our summer visits. I would remain there all morning sometimes, my feet dangling over the edge as I sat dropping pebbles until I heard a distant plop. Often I would return grinning, my bare legs crisscrossed with tiny cuts from my adventures, much to the consternation of my doting mother who would undoubtedly sigh, shake her head and then apply just enough antiseptic to make me want to scream. I never did, though.

I had often imagined I could see eyes there in the depths, glistening beneath the waters, looking up at me through the lattice of the rusted iron grate which prevented me from clambering down the shaft. They terrified and fascinated in equal measure. I fashioned many stories to account for their presence. Mother seemed resigned to let these fantasies run their course.

They persevered though, through angst-ridden adolescence. As an adult, I made tales of terror my stock in trade. The moderate fame granted me suited my quiet lifestyle well. Whilst I never 'made it big', they offered me a creative outlet after long days battling with support calls and the utter mundanity of office life. I was only really content when I closed my own eyes and saw those others staring back at me, unlidded and unblinking. Sometimes there was only a pair of them, staring at me over what I perceived to be a vast gulf of cold damp darkness. At other times, more would open to me. Tens, hundreds even. Watching. Waiting. Hungry.

I went back to that garden many times and not just to visit my grandmother. I even stayed there one summer when she was bedridden after a fall, and I was nursing a bad break up and all the dramatic fallout that usually entails. Each time I went to the well and looked down, rapt in the unknowns of its depths. Always those eyes stared back at me, through me, beyond me. I even spoke to them on occasions, whispering lonely thoughts, dark secrets, hopes and dreams. I like to think that, somehow, they listened, that that's somehow how I got my first big break. A ridiculous notion, surely, but everything I am now I attribute to those slivers of light winking at me from the depths of the well, penetrating the cold iron lattice of the grate and up, up and away to the light of day and the tranquility of that overgrown garden.

Now, with the sad death of my beloved grandmother, the property was mine. I had been signing copies of my latest novel at a book fair when I heard. I had been so caught up in the fame of my new life that I didn't even know she had been struggling with cancer for two years. I tried not to let that detachment get to me, but I carried that guilt through the funeral in late autumn all the way through to signing the deeds in early spring the year after, right up to the moment I drove up to the house in the family Oldsmobile.

I was shocked how much it had changed over the years. Perhaps my memory was playing tricks on me. I cast my mind back to the distant summer days of my youth, kicking my way fearlessly through the long grasses, turning over rocks to find new bugs to torment mother with. The sun warmed my back as I watched my younger self on his bold adventure. Simpler, easier times, before the weight of the world and work took their toll.

Once I had taken inventory and had a list of everything I would need to purchase at the local store, I decided to set out on one further adventure of my own, to the furthest recess of the estate where the ancient, crumbling structure of the stone well resided. I had in mind to stare down the well once more, to gaze unafraid into the inky depths and find those eyes looking back at me once more.

Armed only with a rusty pair of secateurs, I cut a swathe through the thicket. It took me over two hours to make good my passage, by which time the sun was already dimming and the pale moon had risen to claim the heavens in its place. Finally, I reached it, thirsty and exhausted. I leant on it momentarily to catch my breath and then peered over the edge as I had done in my youth.

Nothing gazed back. There were no eyes in the depths watching me. I turned and made ready to return to the solitude of the house.

It was only later that I realized two things which haunt me to this day. Firstly, the grate which once covered the well had no longer been there. Secondly, that the grate was never there to prevent me from falling in. It was to prevent the watcher from climbing out.

The night I spent in that forsaken place was my first in many years. It would also be my last. It remains, boarded and bare, a legacy I am too afraid to claim. For I had already gazed into that abyss and remain deathly afraid that one day it will find me and gaze back.

Time's Up

When I take the opportunity to recall the manifold curios hoarded by my grandpa, one in particular is always first in my thoughts. Even to recall it now causes such shivers that I reach for a pick-me-up with trembling hands. I will tell you the tale of it, for as you will come to learn, this was no common curio, no mere mundane memento. It was a thing of such dread that, many years later, I still lay at nights unable to sleep, listening to the rhythmic patter of rain upon the roof, too fearful to slumber, its face forever burned into my soul.

The object in question was a large floor clock which, we later understood, was purchased on the very day my grandfather was born. Too big for a shelf, it stood on the hall floor, casting a long shadow over the black and white check marble tiles. Perhaps a little ostentatious for its surroundings, it nevertheless became a talking point at every family gathering. In those early days, we thought little of it. When we were young, grandfather would pick us up in his spindly arms and lift us to the face so that we could peer at the workings and wind it up, It was taller than he was even before he became bent with age and he would lift our small frames high above his head and get us to turn the mechanism that kept the clock ticking.

The mechanism kept it ticking. That's what he told us. As I stare at it now, its luminous face casting an eerie light over my sparse lodgings, I wonder if that was ever really the case.

Ninety years. That was the eventual span of my grandfather's life: Throughout that life he became more and more fixated on that clock, which he called his treasure and his prize and occasionally his precious. Every Sunday without fail we would visit with our parents. Every Sunday without fail, he would have us wind the clock and then sit back in his rocking chair, seemingly mesmerized by the swing of the pendulum and the rhythmic tick-tock-tick-tock which echoed throughout the house. No other timepieces were permitted in the place; he strictly forbade it. My parents pandered to that simple but disturbing whim; they found it quaint, charming even. I found it irritating. I longed to know why, but I only ever visited with my parents and whenever I came close to asking the question, worried and frantic looks were exchanged. When later we drove home, there were often harsh words. I did not know then what they were afraid of. I don't even really understand it all now.

I took the opportunity once to visit grandpa on my own. I think I was in my mid-teens at the time and rebelling against anything I could find. He was surprised but glad to see me and ushered me through into the kitchen. While he doddered around - arranging a circle of biscuits on a plate, boiling the kettle, scrabbling for tea bags in a corner cupboard - I steeled myself to ask the question, but found it could not escape my lips. Every sound in that kitchen - the clatter of mugs, the hisses of steam from the stovetop kettle, the rustling of packets -

149

was prompted by an ominous tick from the clock in the hall. I felt sheepish even at the rebellion of wearing my digital watch and pulled down my sleeve hastily before he turned round, embarrassed both that he might see it and at my own cowardly climbdown. He looked at me in that moment and knew. He peered down through furrowed brow and bushy eyebrows and cleared his throat.

"You want to know about the clock, don't you?"

I nodded.

"You can't fool me. Your dad, he never asked. He wound that clock for me for years until your hands were big enough to turn the mechanism. Never asked why., Good kid he was to me and your gran, but incurious. Not you, eh?"

I squirmed, regretting ever coming here, and sipped at my tea.

"It speaks to me, that clock. It knows me. Did you know that? When I married your gran, it knew. Chimed the moment I crossed the threshold. Twenty-four straight chimes. Scared her nearly to death, but she soon laughed after. Thought it was a sign of good luck. Well, we had that, all right. For twenty-four years straight, we had that."

I sat, dumbfounded, not sure what to say. I decided it was best not to say anything.

"Every tick, every tock, I know. It's all I need to listen to. It's what it wants me to listen to. It has shared in my joy, it has shared in my grief, A constant companion throughout the years. Could you ever find one so faithful? Not my wife, not my dog, not even my own children, No, The clock always comes first, And what does it ask in return,

150

really? Just a hand to wind it once a week. That's all."

I hoped that was all it really wanted. I was imaginative at that age and did not wonder how it was that a clock might have wants and desires. I left grandpa soon after that, with two chocolate digestives in my pocket and more questions that I knew I would never have answered.

As I grew older, we visited grandpa less often. But when we did, I always looked at the clock as if it was a living thing, as if there was something there that was reaching out to me. Every week I still wound it at my grandpa's command, even though it scared me to do so. Its face became like a nightmare to me; luminous, ominous, still there as a parting image when I closed my eyes, haunting my daydreams and nightmares alike. I heard the ticking in my head, constant, relentless. Other noises became a torture to me. I started to fail at school; the teachers' comments charting a gradual decline in my faculties, sparking rows with my parents which only brought further pain and gloom as I receded into a world of my own.

It was a rare visit many years later on his birthday that became the turning point. We trouped up as a family as we did in my youth, the car full of cases containing all we would need to spend the night at grandpa's house. I had accepted the invite with a mixture of trepidation and fascination. The clock had not moved; had not even stopped. It loomed long shadows over the hallway as it ever had, the strangely placed rocking chair opposite it in the hall. An evening feast was had, with as much merriment as could be mustered, and we turned in for the evening.

It rang and alarmed in the dead of the night. That alarm had not sounded for many years. I had only heard it once before and knew now what it foretold. The time had come to say goodbye.

As we stood round his bedside, he pleaded quietly to be taken downstairs to see his beloved clock once again. Mother and father looked aghast but willing to comply. As his life seconds were numbering, they faltered. In the hall, all I could hear was a soft and muffled chime. And then, silence.

He left it to me in his will. Father looked perplexed; mother looked worried. I didn't want it. I had seen a glimpse of the obsession it had brought out in grandpa. I was deadly afraid of it, but even more afraid somehow of defying his wishes.

Now it sits in the single room which I laughingly call my home. I've taken myself as far away from other people as the modern world will allow. I still hear the ticking in my head, imagine the gentle swaying of the pendulum forcing my gaze. I have opened that clock a thousand times, inspected every component, taken it apart over and over and then replaced its parts with a grim fascination. Nothing I could do would make it start again. Nothing I could do would make the ticking stop in my head. I don't know why I am so afraid of it. I don't know why it haunts me so.

It has not sounded a beat since the last day in that old house. It stopped short, never to go again when the old man died.

The Children Know

Old Mary Pickham was the most uncharitable soul that ever did walk the gaslit streets of London. She stooped as she stepped, she swore at each chore, she hated as she waited.

It was her lot in life to be the sole caretaker of the parish orphanage and workhouse, an occupation which gave her no satisfaction in life, but which gave opportunities aplenty to inflict her own particular brand of cruelty on her charges with relish - and with very little oversight.

The children were all bundled up for Christmas Eve and 'playing' in the snow of the little courtyard at the front of the building, behind the locked iron gates which prevented them from getting ideas over their head like running away. Usually, the children of this age over which she had been granted control would be huddled up inside rag picking, which is as unappealing a task as it sounds but one deemed by the parish to be suitable for youngsters of that age. Occasionally a sweep would come by and take one of the smaller boys as an apprentice, guaranteeing him a life of ashen misery and an early death. Picking through rags, sorting, stitching, and unstitching, was the best work for small hands, tiring as it was and leading to problems with eyesight when performed under the light of only the three candles old Mary would permit for their use. Still, it usually kept them quiet enough that she didn't have to raise a slipper or belt to them very

153

often, leaving her to get slowly sotted on gin as she supervised them from the little rocking chair next to the fireplace.

Occasionally, one of the cursed urchins would find something interesting in the pile of rags. Then they would begin to smile and laugh among themselves, which was something that above all else old Mary could not abide. Her life had only been sorrow and hardship, why should others be allowed even a modicum of joy in theirs? When this happened, she rose in a drunken stupor and set about them with the heaviest and most punishing implements to hand - a slipper, a frying pan, a rolling pin - chasing and beating and berating them until, in fear, they relented and knuckled down again.

On this occasion, though, she had had enough of their noise altogether and banished them outside, locking the door solidly behind her. Perhaps one of them would freeze to death in the snow-filled courtyard or slip on the ice and break a bone. That would teach them, It didn't matter anyway - she couldn't hear them from where she sat. Out of sight, out of mind.

Most of the children were engaged in building a snowman in the middle of the courtyard. The eldest of them, Douglas, even made the joke that he would be a fine companion for old Mary, being just as cold as she was. This elicited a little laughter from the crowd so Douglas - who was on a roll now - pulled out a top hat from under his threadbare coat and placed it ceremoniously on the snowman's head, doffing his own cap when the task was done.

"Upon my word! Here is a fine gentleman to call upon our own Mary and take her away from this life of misery!" The little group of children laughed again, secure in the knowledge that Mary would probably be stone cold drunk by now or asleep in her chair.

"Where did you get that hat?" That question came from Jemima, whose perpetually grubby face was now red-cheeked from working outside in the cold yard. "It's a bit la-de-dah for our usual take."

"It came to us this morning from old man Moreton at the undertakers. Reckon as how he might have put it in the pile accidentally. But still, finders keepers! And our gentleman caller shall have only the best when he pays a visit to old Mary this evening!" Each of them agreed that in order to win over Mary, he would have to be a jolly soul indeed. They doubted such a thing was even possible. Each of them cursed her under their breath for making their wretched life even more wretched. If Mary herself was full of hate, that hate was at least equaled amongst those in her charge. Secretly, they hoped something would happen that would take her away from them, whether that was a fine gentleman come to woo her or something more sinister.

Their activity was almost instantaneously broken up by the sweary shouts of their overseer telling them their soup was ready. Mary looked out at the mess they'd made in the yard and what they'd built. Cursing under her breath and deciding she was too old to deal with any of this, she decided she would make them clear it up on Christmas morning. That would teach them.

One by one they filed silently back inside, with several of them getting whacks on the backside as they passed Mary, merely for having the insolence to bring in the snow on their bare feet. Douglas reached the door but turned around briefly and bowed theatrically to the snowman in the courtyard who had given them a moment of fun amid their life of misery.

***

That night, Mary made sure all the kids were securely locked inside for the evening and took off to the local hostelry for several hot gin toddies before returning late, swaying on her bandy legs and cussing her meagre shawl which whipped around her thin frame, buffeted by the strong wind which appeared to have come from out of nowhere. Her legs were tired, and her brain addled. All she wanted to do was to sleep.

It seemed like Mary was not going to get what she wanted.

The old iron gates creaked open as she rattled the key in the hole, then clanged shut behind her as she set the chains back in place. Then, there was silence. She made her way slowly across the courtyard, cursing the cold grey air which took so much warmth from her frail form, cursing her fate at having to perform such a duty as taking care of these unruly and unkempt young tykes and cursing her eyesight because she swore she saw something move out of the corner of her eye where there shouldn't be something moving.

It came upon her suddenly, with a swift flurry of snow and a swifter flurry of fists. She recoiled from the strength of those blows but also from the chill of its touch which left great red welts swelling on her skin wherever those blows landed. In a last-ditch effort to save her wretched hide, Mary Pickham tried to scream and run toward the door, trying to get into the relative warmth of her workhouse quarters and away from this sudden hail of abuse. She failed at the first. She tried to call out, but her icy breath froze on her lips and sealed her mouth shut. The form continued to lope towards her, thrashing the air before it with its icy fists as it advanced. Now pressed against the door, there was nothing she could do against its assault. It loomed over her, its unfeeling eyes black as coal and its breath cold as the dead of winter. Unballing its fist to reveal long fingers, each as sharp and deadly as an icicle, it began to rake those claws over her prone body. When it was done, it removed the top hat with a flourish and gave her a long, deep bow as her the red of her blood mingled with the white of the snow and began to trickle away from the door, running pink rivulets into the grey slush accumulating at the corners of the brickwork.

The bloody pulp which was all that remained of Old Mary was discovered the next morning by a visiting tradesman, concerned that she had not replied to his many shouts from the gate. A dutiful and fastidious soul, he raised the alarm and summoned the local constabulary to take care of the investigation, though not before removing from the

157

coffers 'that which was owed to me right and proper by the cantankerous old witch'.

Of her assailant, there was no trace. When the police had finished clearing the snowdrift in the workhouse courtyard, all they found was a corn cob pipe, a button, and a battered top hat. Inspector Newcross picked the hat up and brushed off the light dusting of snow. He turned it over slowly in his cold fingers, looking for a name or a maker's mark written into the lining. It was a good quality item. Not something he'd expected to see in this establishment. He decided to keep it as a perk of the job.

The inspector arranged for a temporary custodian to take care of the building and the remaining orphans until the parish council could find a more permanent solution. He knew that the chances of them picking a kindly soul who actually liked children was miniscule. There was nothing here to warm his heart, just never-ending poverty and misery. Standing at the wrought iron gates awaiting their arrival, he contemplated the words they had all spoken under questioning. He had never encountered such a conspiracy of silence except among the most hard-bitten criminals of the capital. There was one phrase, though, which they had all uttered in shared whispers. Damn, but it almost sounded like a veiled threat.

"He'll be back again someday."

Whatever had happened here the previous night would remain in the unsolved files of Scotland Yard. But Inspector Newcross was sure of one thing. The children knew.

Who's Afraid

On the first night of the hunter's moon, it took my youngest brother.

We had all made our claim to farmsteads in Virginia and lived close by to each other as brothers should. You never met anyone as carefree and happy as my youngest brother. He was not a natural farmer, but he did love nature. He would spend all day lazing on his porch and gazing up at the birds as they flew across the cornfields.

And in one night, he was lost to me.

In truth, I do not know fully what came for us. We had heard rumors of a haunting presence in the woods, but had never seen it up close. At night, the wind would howl outside but we were as safe as houses. Or so we thought. This is not to say that I was idle; I had ordered several books of local folklore which I studied assiduously when the hard work of the day was done. I wanted to be ready.

I cannot say the same for my brothers. Routinely they chastised me for studying when I could be idling my evenings away swimming in the lake or playing the fiddle on the porch. Their summers were merry and bright, mine was full of threat and worry. If what I read was true, we were in big trouble. My brothers did not want to believe in the histories I had collected. They were determined to stay put, as was I. We had too much to lose.

Then one night, it came. The wind rose from a low whisper across the lakeside reeds until it reached fever pitch. I dared not open the window but stared through the pane in horror as I saw the face of our nocturnal villain. Its form was huge, evil and somewhat lupine in countenance. I heard it howl at the wind; I heard the wind howl back in a unity of cacophony. The wind rose to a full gale, sweeping across the fields at its master's bidding; a fetid, rancid breath that tore through the whole valley with a rapacious appetite. I bolted my door and shuttered the windows, I hoped that my brothers had the good sense to do the same.

It was not to be.

For precious moments the howling abated, only to be replaced by a different sound. I hope you never have to listen to the drawn-out death rattle of one of your own close kin. I hope that never happens to anyone. I knew from the first moment of that high squeal that he would not survive. Never once did I move from my position, safe inside the circle of stones I had prepared on the floor. I bit my tongue and let the tears flow down my cheeks as his life ebbed. But I did not move, for I knew that to do so would be to invite disaster. By my beard, I would not risk letting that horror inside where it might devour me.

We buried him the next day on the shore of the lake. Neither my remaining brother nor I wanted to talk very much that day. We dug, we hugged, and we parted. I asked if he wanted to stay with me. I knew the lore. I had the protections. Inconceivably, he shrugged off the suggestion. Maybe he wanted to be alone with his thoughts. I suppose I did too, otherwise I would have been stronger in my insistence.

The next night, it came for him. At first there was nothing but the crickets and the bubbling creek to disturb our sleep. Then the moon shuddered bright silver through the clouds and shone upon that solitary, hungry form. I watched through a crack in the window. It stood on its hind legs, tall and terrible, and let out a low mournful howl which set my very soul on edge. I withdrew, checked the traps and the protective stones, and squatted in case it came knocking. At the last moment, I called out to my brother - as loud as I could before the gathering storm made it impossible - begging him to join me in safety. There was no reply.

Dare I move? Dare I open the door and race to his aid? To lose one brother was enough tragedy for our family. I should use the remaining time to fetch him to safety. I went to the door, unbolted it and called again.

I could see his pale pink face pressed against the window of his log cabin. He knew now that I was right; I swore he even mouthed an apology to me before the shape bound into view, snarling long white teeth and reaching out with vicious claws, thrashing around itself in ecstasy as he brought forth the storm. I closed my eyes, withdrew, and began chanting.

I never saw my brother again. In the morning, when the land was no longer dark and the wind no longer came whistling across the plain, I left the safety of my stones and opened the door. Of my brothers' houses there was no sign. The wind had raised them whole from their foundations and carried them away in its fury. I stood rigid in fear and grief alike. I knew that tonight it would come for me. Would I stand firm and not let it in? There was a part of me, and is still, that wanted it to be over, for me to rejoin my kin in the hereafter.

If it should be that you have discovered this note in the ruins of a stone Virginian farmstead, or perhaps in a collection of old documents in a distant dusty library - a curio from a place and a time long forgotten - know that it came for me also and that I was afraid.

The Mirror Crack'd

My name is Medusa. They tell me I'm ugly.
Monstrous, even. Looking at my sisters, nobody
would ever consider them beauties, but they insist
I'm worse.

So much worse.

We don't have any mirrors in the house, so it's
impossible to check. No visitors either. I only have
their opinion to rely on. As cruel and capricious as
my ugly sisters are, who am I to disbelieve them? I
do check occasionally in the waters of the little
brook that flows at the end of the garden, or in the
surfaces of the shiny black stones that litter
Sarpedon. It's difficult to describe what I see when
nature distorts my image so. I therefore rely on my
sisters for verification. They rely on me for
everything else.

They say I'm so ugly that any man who looks at
me would be frozen in horror. My countenance is so
unnaturally hideous that any suitor would be
petrified by my mere presence. This is not what
directly puts them off, you understand. What puts
them off are the rumors. People might make the
journey to Sarpedon to gawp at a freak. A tale to tell
their companions. *"At the edge of the world, I once
saw..."* Taverns are full of such stories, so I
understand. I've never been that far away from the
house, so I can only imagine what that's like. But a
story that says I'm so hideous that people wouldn't

survive seeing me? That only attracts one type of visitor, and they're rare. So rare. And that's just what I need to escape this life of drudgery, of misery, of loneliness.

I need a hero.

Heroes usually slay monsters like me. Like my sisters. Look, one approaches now. I can feel the prickle of anticipation at his arrival. A prince! My own sweet prince! Euryale and Stheno are ecstatic. They're miserable as well, I can understand that. But it's difficult to feel empathy for them when they take all that misery out on me.

The preparations mostly involve making sure the Greek prince feels welcome in the home when he visits. Naturally, I won't be allowed on the premises while he's there.

Naturally.

Once he arrives, I am sent off to the cave with a loaf of bread and a pitcher of water. They say they'll collect me when he's left. I hope they leave with him.

He avoids the hut.

Makes straight for the cave.

I can feel him coming, my snaky hair stands on end and my neck prickles.

Don't make me do this...

I can't see him! Why can't I see him? I can make out his footsteps in the sand, hear the clattering of his armor. His shield is polished bright, sending rays of sunlight into the darkest recesses of my hiding place.

"Go away!"

164

I dare to speak, even though it gives away my place.

"There's nothing here for you! Only death!" I try to warn him, but the echoes of the cave amplify my voice, make it sound threatening. I curse under my breath.

"Stop hiding, monster!" Now he's given away his place too. Not that I have any way of taking advantage of that. I only have one weapon…

I stand up. Move forward boldly.

He's averting his gaze so that he doesn't look at me directly. He knows. He's come prepared. He's canny, this one. Brave, even. He looks into his shield to find my location. Yes, I can see you now, hero. Since you're clearly not here to rescue me, there's only one role left to assume.

I am a monster.

I step forward and hiss at him menacingly. At least, I hope it's menacingly.

He moves to strike. I dodge.

Everything now happens quickly. I catch a glimpse of myself in the mirror of his shield and stop suddenly in my movement.

It's the first time I've seen myself properly, without the refractions and distortions and lies that the streams and stones and sisters use to make me doubt myself.

I'm not a monster.

I'm fucking beautiful.

Gorgeous, not gorgon.

And in that moment, he knows it too. Lowers his defenses and stares right at me.

165

Say what you like about me - and I've heard all the rumors - but the male gaze is more deadly and debilitating than anything the poets ever said about poor Medusa. I quiver under it.

He drops his shield. The mirrored surface shatters to the cave floor, a thousand shards of his reflected glory and my reflected pain. He freezes dead in his tracks. Not because he's petrified by my monstrosity. Oh, no. Because he's captivated by my beauty. He can't move. He's standing there dumbfounded, mouth agape, eyes wide open. Then he falls to his knees. My prince. My hero.

That's the power I have. You want to turn heads? Make men stand and stare? Look at me. I got what you need right here.

Tell No Tales

Gather round, gather round. I'm here to tell a story. You've probably heard parts of it before. Throughout the length and breadth of the bay, this story has been told anew with each rising tide. Every time it is, it varies a little. Small changes are made, embellishments emphasizing local character by those who were at the telling of it, or by those who were at the telling of a telling of it and so on as each tale trickles down like a little stream finding its way to the shore. And each of them does find its own way, though they flow eventually into that self-same sea where these events first happened.

The story goes something like this. I swear by my own experiences of the past three weeks that it's all true, so help me God.

Somewhere in the bay is a hidden island lost in banks of mist and surrounded by dangerous shoals. On that island is a vast amount of buried treasure. Every pirate captain in their day once berthed on its only safe beach, accompanied by the newest members of their crew, oblivious to what was about to happen. These unknowing sailors carried a chest of ill-gotten gains to a lonely cave or a hidden cove or a turn in the river, where there lies a deep pit at the base of an old, gnarled tree. When they laid the last of the treasure in that pit, a face appeared in the bark, green eyes glowing with malevolent energy. Branches reached down and grabbed them, hurling them into the sacrificial pit where quick-running sands and fast-flowing waters seeped over them and buried them alive. Then the tree screamed like the gull in the storm, a cry that mingled with the wind in the dead wood of its branches or the waves shrilling on the outer beach. Even the cruelest of buccaneers shivered as they heard that wail. Yet each captain knew that their treasure was safe, its whereabouts protected by an ancient evil, paid for with lost souls and the silence of the grave.

Spooky, huh? I was perfectly placed to recall the tales that were told in tavern and manor alike, and how could I not be? I have been writing and performing variations on the tale since I first heard it. I had sought out every account I could find and confabulated them into stirring scripts of comedy, tragedy, morality and horror alike. That summer our performances were praised in every parlor, toasted in every tavern. No one had a greater collection of these stories than I. We sailed in the wake of these tales and for a while were the singular sensation of the summer. After several years languishing at the bottom of every playbill, it seemed we had finally found our fortune. Even when innumerable encores tested us to the point of exhaustion, we managed to shine throughout the night as bright as the stars themselves. I never considered for one moment that there was truth in those tales. Until a certain map came into my possession: the result of a sotted quartermaster and a lost wager.

The seasonal performances had ended at that point and had left us with a reasonable sum which we could have invested in a new play or idled away in luxury until the day our indolence exceeded our funds. But we wanted more. And I had in my possession the key not only to this great treasure, but the story that came with it. A story we could live if we were bold enough. A story I could retell. This story.

We spent three days arguing about what to do and a matter of hours finding a captain with equal measures of greed and foolhardiness who might see our dreams fulfilled. We tramped the gangplank of The Hasty Maiden without a care in the world, our heads swimming with the tang of salt and adventure.

Now, Captain Juanita Argentina was a harsh woman with a harsh crew, but cheap, willing, and available. Too willing, perhaps. That should have been our first clue. We had been uncomfortable about showing her the map until we were underway, but now we unfolded it in her cabin, and all looked at it intently.

"Three days sail south along the coast, two tacking to the southwest and a further day on the open waves. That should do it. We'll make landfall in no time: the winds will favour us outward bound but the return voyage will be trickier." She looked up. "Any of you ever sailed before?" She did not look surprised when we all replied in the negative, merely dismissed us with a wave of her tattooed hand and strode out on the deck to shout orders to her band of miscreants and misfits.

I'll spare you the details of the journey. I can see you're all familiar with such things. Suffice to say that we enjoyed the trip immensely, got in the way

169

of operations and generally made a nuisance of ourselves. For the most part, I was fascinated by ship life and dedicated myself to learning everything I could of my new environment as fodder for future fantasies. The sea behaved, the winds were with us and nothing unfortunate occurred. I can tell from your mumblings that you think that in itself is unusual. But what were we to know? We were actors, not sailors. Our waves were ribbons of blue and white, our boat an upturned table. Despite initial appearances, the captain ran a tight ship and we arrived at the island on the day appointed and not a moment before or after. That, of course, is where the adventure began in earnest.

Once we had navigated the eerie fog which surrounded the place and narrowly avoided the shoals only by virtue of them being marked on our map, the captain called for us. We were to join her and her alone in a rowing boat and make our way to the place marked. The crew would remain to take care of the ship and make repairs to the rigging in readiness for our return. She bade us carry a small chest down to the boat. Since she didn't tell us not to look inside, we did. There were three small shovels, an axe, a good length of rope and a barrel of gunpowder. When we asked, she grinned. "That damned tree will never see what's coming." She spoke this with a degree of smug satisfaction that it mollified any reticence we had. That was our second warning. It's difficult, you see, even when you know the story, to see it when you're living it. It's like what they say inland about wood and trees.

There was a slow rise at the edge of the shore, and we picked our way toward it over the hot sand. The sun beat down on our backs as the beach became spotted with clumps of grass and reeds. Small pools of brackish water spotted the marshland just over that rise, shrouded in a low hanging mist which clung to us with clammy hands as we tried to get bearings from our map of the island. There were few trees here at all and none of them seemed to be in the right place. This did not slow the captain's pace one jot. Whenever she turned back to admonish us for moving too slowly, what little of her face we could see between hat and throat seemed locked in a foreboding grimace which did nothing to raise our cheer or allay our fears.

We spent a full three hours crossing that marsh, leeches on our legs and flies on our face. By the time we reached a low hillock of dry ground, we were exhausted. And there, lonely as a lost soul, was the dead tree shown on the old quartermaster's map. What sighs of relief we made! The end of an arduous trek, the promise of wealth, the malodorous fumes of the marsh, they each made us giddy in different ways.

"Here it is. Get those shovels out and show us what you're made of!" None of us noticed the captain's voice dropping a register. None of us hesitated to start digging. We were full of the wonder of the moment, resurgent after all the energy spent trudging through saltmarsh. We didn't even notice when her eyes flashed green for a moment. A trick of the light, perhaps. We were used to those on the stage. The first thing we noticed was

171

when the branches of the tree began to move a moment later, creaking into a facsimile of life. Rotted roots reached for our ankles even as thick, knobbled branches began to lash out at our arms and faces.

The captain was laughing full-throated now, a raucous racket which came from somewhere beyond this earth, her head bent back in gloating triumph. Three more unwary souls for her infernal bargain.

That's when I rushed forward unsuspectingly, barreled into her and knocked her backward into the waterlogged pit. She hung mid-air for a moment and with wide-eyed horror saw the moment of her undoing. Pale figures gathered above her around the pit mouth: ghosts of those who had been killed here, sacrificed to this ancient effigy of wickedness beneath whose roots lay wealth unimaginable. As she opened her mouth to plead for mercy, a pale figure rose from the depths and wrapped its cold fingers around her neck. More followed, spectral clammy hands grasping at her but ignoring us. As the captain gasped for breath, the pit collapsed around her, burying her in a watery grave. The tree fell silent.

We rested there awhile until we realized we should get back and signal the ship, to try and explain what had happened to the captain. When we reached the beach, however, there was no sign of it. We slept under the stars and vowed to tackle our mounting problems in the morning.

Now, I hate to be a spoilsport but here is the lay of things. We spent three days on that island doing nothing but digging with those shovels and drinking our fill of coconut water. At the end of that time, we still hadn't found any sign of buried treasure. Not a pearl or a sapphire or a single piece of eight. I tell you now, there's no reward to be had there. Danger, sure. A curse, absolutely. But no treasure. When we were rescued on the fourth day by a passing merchantman, we disembarked at the first port and vowed never to take to sea again or speak of what had happened.

It might seem strange, then, that I'm telling you this now. Truth is, we sunk all our funds in that venture, and it came to nothing. I only ask that you reach into your pockets for a modest amount of coin, to ease the aching in this storyteller's throat and afford me a few minor comforts. I thank you.

***

It was a little later, as I stood alone on the dock, that I was approached by an elderly seafaring gentleman who had been in the crowd earlier.

"That's a fine story. It's a shame about the treasure. Just a story, right?"

I nodded. He seemed to want to say more.

"It's just that I couldn't help noticing that doubloon you paid for your meal with. Reckon as that's an old, old, coin. One that might come from an old, old, story."

I turned to him and winked. We smiled at each other in the dead of night, the only noise the gentle lapping of waves.

Then I stared at him, long and hard and deep, my eyes suddenly glowing a hideous shade of green, my voice a harsh screech heard throughout the

173

years. I shrieked loud and long like a gull across the
bay, louder than the ocean itself.

The Name of the Star

I write this missive in the understanding that whosoever discovers it may comprehend the summary of my research and then seek to repeat it, perhaps with more caution than I. The knowledge herein contains the secret name of the star, which I believe to be unknown to the guild who would do everything in their power to obtain it. I shall start with a little history.

The liberator fell from a star.

Whatever shape it took, how it presented itself in its brief interactions with our people, is apparently lost to history. That may not be entirely accurate. It is equally likely that the guild is sitting on that information and not sharing it. That has happened a lot since the arrival of the liberator. Those that were present at the event - the oldest among us of whom precious few remain - have but the vaguest of memories which can be awakened only out of earshot of the guild and their network of spies. Even then, it often takes strong liquor, or a hefty bribe of gold and I am currently lacking in both.

What happened, then, was this. The liberator is called such because the craft they arrived in happened to land - evidently accidentally - on the dwelling of the one who ruled in those days. That iron fist, that velvet glove, are now relics of our history. The craft of the liberator is not. It squats in the middle of the village, surrounded now by a high fence of barbed wire and patrolled by agents of the guild who will not allow others to plunder its secrets. One tyranny was exchanged for another.

The guild moved quickly once the liberator had left on their own journey and left the craft behind. From the accounts I have managed to glean, and from stolen glances through the wire, it resembles one of our own dwellings, larger in size but fashioned similarly of wood. Whilst it is not whitewashed in our traditional fashion, the timbers are from trees not unknown to these parts. Curiosity compelled many in the early days to investigate the scene of our liberation, but the guild decided that the contents should only be studied by experts.

Their experts.

'KEEP OUT' signs were erected, guards were posted. Before his passing, my father used to tell me that several local households still had artefacts of the liberator that they had themselves, in turn, liberated from the craft. These were held in high esteem, often placed in prominence on a table as a talking piece or given pride of place on a mantle for good luck. A few folk marveled at them, others sought to understand them. The guild sought only to suppress them. One night, their agents knocked down doors on every house where artefacts were said to dwell and confiscated the whole bunch. Their tyrannical takeover was complete, or so they thought.

That night, the resistance began. First in glances exchanged, then in whispers stolen, then in meetings held out of sight and out of mind. The guild always broke these up when they found out about them. Punishment for attendance was severe. The resistance faltered but did not die. What they did was begin to pray.

In hidden glades and lost caves, wherever the resistance met, they offered prayers to the liberator. They begged for another chance for freedoms they had neither the power nor courage to win themselves. What artefacts remained amongst the population were set on plinths and altars as objects of adulation and genuflection. Crude wooden replicas of the craft were fashioned in silence, left roofless so that when within, worshippers could gaze up at the night sky and hope, dream, pray for salvation. The stars, in their turn, merely twinkled in mute acceptance of their newfound supplicants.

Nothing came.

In more academic circles such as my father's - and now mine - there were heated discussions which went beyond the blind faith professed by the multitude. How had the craft arrived? From which star did it originate? Theories abounded, ideas debated, and plans discarded. Eventually, these vague plans coalesced around a single sentiment: Could the star be reached? Then, in refinement, *how* could the star be reached? If the craft could make it here, what would it take for us to make the return journey? All of this was done in the hushed corners of libraries and without the benefit of those benefactors we had relied on in the past, all so that the guild would notice the activities taking place under their very noses.

Since it is forbidden to possess star charts of the night sky, we made them anew from scratch, from observation, from memory, hiding them in plain sight on the skins of paper lanterns which only illuminated them when they themselves were lit up. The star at the center of these charts was the one from which we believed the liberator had originated.

Tonight, I will make that journey. It is a further distance by far than any of our people have ever travelled and yet this is the first time in many years that I feel totally unafraid.

I will leave my own cottage under cover of darkness, sure of my mission. Sneak past the guild guardsmen, their halberds crossed under the 'KEEP OUT' sign on the imposing gate before the craft of the liberator, the barbs of wire furled over it glistening in the low moonlight. Tiptoe my way to the far glade, beyond the road to the west. From there, I should be able to hear the resistance movement chanting in unison and pass between them as they call forth the name of the liberator in their throes of ecstasy: "Doh - roh - ti, Doh - roh - ti!", their intonations guttural, the words alien to my ears yet somehow comforting. I have watched this ceremony a thousand times and it always sets my senses on edge as they prostrate themselves before the facsimile of the craft which they face in worship.

I shall journey to that distant star and find another liberator to assist us. Else, I will become the liberator of that star, perhaps, and be placed among them as a king, to rule in benevolence rather than fear.

If you have found this, it is likely that I have not returned, lost on the long journey into the void of the heavens or in turbulent somnolence in the realms between dreams and nightmares. I know not which. I only beg, dear reader, that you continue my work. It is for this reason I leave you with the name of the star as spoken by the liberator.

"Kan-Zazz."

The Last Laugh

A man calls the doctor. He says he's angry and depressed. He says that life seems harsh and cruel, and he feels all alone in a threatening world.

The doctor says, 'For that, the treatment is simple. The great clown, Pagliacci, is in town tonight. Go and see him. That should pick you up.'

The man looks down at the murdered clown at his feet, blood still oozing among the smudged white make up and the bright yellow frock.

He hangs up on the doctor. He drops the bloodstained knife. Then he laughs. A maniacal, hellish laugh that lasts forever.

www.ingramcontent.com/pod-product-compliance
Lightning Source LLC
Chambersburg PA
CBHW011440170626
46807CB00008B/3237